ADVANCE PRAISE FOR *ALL THAT IS SOLID MELTS INTO AIR*:

With shattering grace Giangrande divines catastrophic grief, the redemptive power of ephemeral joys, and the interconnectedness of all things as past and present conflate in terrorism's chaos. Memory becomes balm as life, all life, is porous. Exquisite, devastating, this book *is* a bomb.
—CAROL BRUNEAU, author of *Glass Voices* and *These Good Hands*

An elegy for lost innocence, *All That Is Solid Melts Into Air* is at once extremely sad and exquisitely hopeful. Its hopefulness resides mainly in the stubborn resonance of the quotidian, and in the kind hearts and good wills of those who refuse to accept evil, no matter how often it crashes into their lives. Carole Giangrande has achieved a great deal in this short, beautiful book; confronting the incomprehensible without despair and describing profound grief without sentimentality.
—SUSAN GLICKMAN, author of *The Tale-Teller* and *Safe as Houses*

All That Is Solid Melts into Air is a magical work of literature, brimming with wondrous imagery and subtle threads of the future/present/past entwined in a radiant narrative that will have you feeling Valerie's pain, sensing her confusion and her desire to keep busy while she awaits any news regarding the fate of her loved ones. Her solid world (and the world around her) has melted into air.
—MIRAMICHI READER

All That Is Solid Melts Into Air is above all a compassionate book. Carole Giangrande takes that horrifying day—September 11, 2001—and filters it though the consciousness of a woman, Valerie, whose loved ones are in Manhattan as the crisis unfolds. She doesn't know whether they are dead or alive, and Giangrande is masterful in her

expression of Valerie's surreal state of mind. The book captures with gut-wrenching acuity the anxiety, fear and distress of not only that particular day but of our current social climate as well. No one is safe anymore—was anyone, ever?—and our perceptions rule us: "The truth was that everything you looked at had to pass through the lens of what you imagined you saw. It was up to you to decide what was real." Timely words from a timely book.
—EVA TIHANYI, author of *Flying Underwater: Poems New and Selected* and *The Largeness of Rescue*

In *All That is Solid Melts Into Air,* the language of trauma is made lyrical and evocative in Carole Giangrande's hands so that like her characters, we become witnesses again in our post-9/11 imaginations and hearts. And it is her female protagonist, Valerie, we follow with an empathic blend of dread and hope in the hours before and after the tragedy. Gardener and nurturer of the earth, wife and mother in frantic search of her son, it is Valerie whose fragmented memories, dreams and premonitions we decipher while Giangrande skillfully weaves us back and forth in time and place. As we uncover Valerie's intertwining life stories of love and loss and shuttle from the richly depicted landscape of Saint-Pierre to a devastated Lower Manhattan, we recognize "how precious human conjunctions are" for all those of us left behind. A riveting and reflective read of the cumulative moments that mark a life.
—CAROL LIPSZYC, author of *The Saviour Shoes and Other Stories*

All That Is Solid
Melts
Into Air

All That Is Solid Melts Into Air

a novel
Carole Giangrande

inanna poetry & fiction series

INANNA PUBLICATIONS AND EDUCATION INC.
TORONTO, CANADA

We gratefully acknowledge the support of the Canada Council for the Arts and the Ontario Arts Council for our publishing program. We also acknowledge the financial support of the Government of Canada through the Canada Book Fund.

Cover artwork: cubehero, "The Dissolving City," 2014, digital artwork, 1920 x 1080. http://cubehero.deviantart.com
Cover design: Val Fullard

All That Is Solid Melts Into Air is a work of fiction. All the characters and situations portrayed in this book are fictitious and any resemblance to persons living or dead — with the exception of historical personages — is purely coincidental. Names and incidents are the products of the author's imagination and historical events are used fictitiously.

Library and Archives Canada Cataloguing in Publication

Giangrande, Carole, 1945–, author
        All that is solid melts into air / Carole Giangrande.

(Inanna poetry & fiction series)
Issued in print and electronic formats.
ISBN 978-1-77133-361-0 (paperback). — ISBN 978-1-77133-362-7 (epub). — ISBN 978-1-77133-363-4 (kindle) — ISBN 978-1-77133-364-1 (pdf)

        I. Title. II. Series: Inanna poetry and fiction series

PS8563.I24A45 2017   C813'.54   C2017-900284-8
                                                  C2017-900285-6

Printed and bound in Canada

Inanna Publications and Education Inc.
210 Founders College, York University
4700 Keele Street, Toronto, Ontario, Canada M3J 1P3
Telephone: (416) 736-5356 Fax: (416) 736-5765
Email: inanna.publications@inanna.ca Website: www.inanna.ca

MIX
Paper from
responsible sources
FSC® C004071

For Judi Engel

There! Out it boomed. First a warning, musical; then the hour,
irrevocable. The leaden circles dissolved in the air. Such fools
we are, she thought.
                                   —Virginia Woolf, *Mrs. Dalloway* (1925)

Remember the ordinary, if you can.
                    — *New York Times* editorial (12 September 2001)

I.

1

A S SHE WALKED UPHILL on Rue Maréchal Foch in the old town of Saint-Pierre, Valerie heard clocks. There were hundreds of them ticking, her ears itching with tiny sounds, as if she'd stepped into a puddle of time, sending up a swarm of minutes and seconds. She stopped walking and glanced at her watch — seven-forty, Mid-Atlantic daylight time. It was a foggy late-summer morning, the steep, narrow street alive with pedestrians edging their way around parked minivans and moving cyclists. If she'd looked southward, back the way she'd come, she'd see *le barachois*, the inlet that sheltered the town's harbour from the Atlantic Ocean. A few days ago she'd arrived at Saint-Pierre, a dot of French soil east of Nova Scotia and south of Newfoundland, a period at the end of a long Canadian sentence. *Not Canada*, Valerie thought. Or her American birthplace. A speck of France in the eye of the sea.

As she inched along the cobbled sidewalk, she heard the sound again, the chatter of dozens of tiny, meshing gears. *Tick-tock, tickety-tock.* She wondered where the sound was coming from, and then she asked herself why clocks couldn't tick together on cue, like a well-conducted choir. She'd read somewhere that time is an illusion. In that case, their randomness wouldn't matter. Valerie noticed a sign a short block from the intersection, right next door to the photo shop. *Horlogerie.*

The clock shop was too far away for such a racket, but as she approached, the sound grew no louder. The shop turned out to be nothing special, with its display window full of conservative gold wristwatches, black leather-banded ones, a few funky pastel styles with fat faces and big hands. She could glimpse larger, noisier clocks inside. Next to the door was a plaque that read *L. Sarazin, Propriétaire.* The door was open, but there was no one behind the counter. The shop was empty.

In the morning fog, the place appeared in a strange light — diffuse and pearly, like the moon through cloud, light dimmed from its long journey across time. Many years ago she'd seen the same luminous softness dusting the ground, sifting through the leaves of dogwoods and sycamores. Pale, eerie beauty, a late-August afternoon before a storm, and she was a child on a wooded street on another island. There at the shaded edges of New York City, a boy her age was sitting on a tree stump, carving a piece of wood with his pocket knife. Matthew was as fair as she was, and as quiet as breath. In her teens, she'd called him Sonny and he'd called her Cloudy, but that was sweet talk and just between the two of them.

Nowadays, Matthew sent her e-mails. *I'm going on vacation today. Please keep me in your prayers.* She didn't pray, so he'd have to make do with buzzing around the edges of her thoughts.

She imagined him as a youth, coming back to her this morning in the form of light. Yet he was a shadowed man, and that would be an odd way to make his presence known. It was his dad who'd tinkered with clocks. On those summer afternoons, as she sat on their back stoop and watched the boy whittle and hum to himself, she'd hear from indoors the wild rattling and bonging of the hours, the tinny noise of minutes and seconds breaking on her ears. The din had unnerved her. Walking alone up Rue Maréchal Foch, Valerie wondered what had become of those clocks. She thought about her husband, Gerard Lefèvre, who was a broadcast journalist and therefore a punctual man. He was a thousand kilometres away from here, covering a Quebec arts fête in New York City.

Quelque chose de différent, he'd said — not the newsbeat. The station already had an arts reporter in the city, but Gerard was political and his producer hoped for some outspoken views on Quebec's nationhood emerging through its art. Gerard was ambivalent about the assignment, but he liked the idea of working in New York. *Would you like to come?* he'd asked Valerie. *We could visit Andre, go see a show.*

Andre was their oldest child, and New York City was her hometown. She'd said no to his invitation because she'd made other plans. Gerard travelled so much and to such war-ridden places that she couldn't imagine a New York story that would interest him. *Bring me a picture*, she'd said.

When her husband would go on assignment, she'd always ask for photos, something to encapsulate the meaning of a place — crumbling stone roads where the Roman army had marched and conquered Britain; the elegant Mostar Bridge in Herzegovina, before it was bombed and destroyed in the nineties. His pictures went beyond his torrent of TV commentary, straight to the haunting of that Roman road by armed ghosts, to the last light that graced the bridge before it fell. He'd find some way of showing her Manhattan that she herself would never have imagined.

* * *

Last night, Gerard had called her. "I've taken some wonderful pictures," he said. "You see how much I think of you?" and she'd felt a pang of longing. He'd stood with Henri, his cameraman, on the observation deck of the city's highest tower, doing commentary, shooting a backgrounder for the evening news, showing Quebecers the grandeur of a city where their finest artists were about to perform. Monday morning — yesterday — Henri had opened his shutter, panning the horizon while Gerard, by his own admission, had been caught up in seeing what was beyond sight and beyond speech. As he spoke to her, Valerie had imagined the sun through his eyes — silver, an oyster's pearl, nudging the eastern sky into a pink iridescence, like the inside of a seashell. He would have tasted the salt air of a childhood holiday in Maine when he'd found a beautiful clamshell and put it in his tin bucket, remembering with his tongue, his skin, his sense of smell, how his mother had admired it. Cherishing these memories, he'd always felt at home near water, loving the words of the ancient king who wrote that *all rivers run to the sea and the sea is never full.* Far below, the two great tidal estuaries of the East River and the Hudson spilled into New York Bay at the tip of Manhattan.

"So let me tell you about my photos," said Gerard.

He'd taken out his camera and walked around the observation deck facing west, the crack of daylight blood red behind him, and then he angled toward the opposite tower and shot the picture. He'd wanted to zoom in on the Brooklyn Bridge, only he couldn't shoot into the sun. "I took it later, from the ground," he told her. He'd asked Andre to scan the photos into his computer. Their son had clients in the tower, and he was never without his laptop. "Tomorrow," Gerard said. "He's promised to send them tomorrow."

Henri filmed her husband in the eerie dawn. It must have been a beautiful sight, a mesh of thin haze floating across the cloudless blue, across the ragtag skyline, above downtown as it yawned and stretched itself into another day. "I imagined you flying to Saint-Pierre," said Gerard, and then across his field of vision came a streak of light, an airplane crossing the blue sky.

* * *

Valerie had grown used to their separateness. It surprised her to learn that Gerard had not. Or maybe he wanted her along because he didn't have a taxing assignment in New York, because he'd thought she might like to see Andre. What took him aback was her single-minded planning, her longing to hike among the flowering plants that thrived on mist and rain. In June he'd gone to the Hague to cover Milosevic, his delivery to the War Crimes Tribunal. While he was gone, she'd booked her flight to Saint-Pierre.

"You have never gone on a trip alone before," he'd said.

"But you have," she'd answered. "Often."

Last night when he called from New York, she told him about the time difference. *Deux heures en avance* — two hours ahead of him. She heard the ticking again and felt uneasy.

2

IN THE WINDOW of the *horlogerie*, Valerie saw her pensive face reflected back, its sunlight breaking through now and again. Her hair was long and ash-blond, tucked under a sun-hat, her backpack slouching on her shoulder. She was tall, with the self-conscious stoop of her teenage years, when she'd imagined her head like a top-heavy sunflower dangling from its stalk. Her eyes were no particular colour—grey on a cloudy day, azure by the sea. "How the world looks from thirty-five thousand feet," said Gerard once, gazing at her. Perhaps she was as fogbound as the weather on these islands.

They'd honeymooned here over thirty years ago, spending a week at the *pension* of his cousin Marguerite. In those days Saint-Pierre was a humble town of shopkeepers and fishermen, its ragged mists too chill and austere for tourism, and it crept into the twenty-first century much the same as it had always been. Valerie didn't care one way or the other. She'd loved the comforting fog, the frailty of this island, its slender hold on life.

"But why would you go to such a place again?" asked Gerard.

"It's a trip to France."

"*D'accord. C'est évident.*" He shrugged.

It was also, Valerie realized, a chance to visit with cousins who she only saw on their occasional trips to Quebec.

Gerard had been a good father, but after Andre and Chantal left home, he gave up his local TV news job to become a freelance correspondent. Sarajevo, Belfast, Haiti — his accounts of a terrorist bombing or a massacre would explode into a rumble of words that shook the house.

"And what did you learn?" she'd ask him.

"What I always learn."

"And that is?"

Gerard would grow quiet. "To be a good witness," he'd say.

He'd grown up in Montreal, troubled by the bombings of the sixties, so impatient with violence that he regarded even moderate *indépendentistes* with disgust. Nor would he speak about the loss of his first love, Ora — not how she'd perished, or even where; not even the fact that she'd died too young. "What I remember, I live," he'd say, as he paid keen attention to the sufferings of innocents in combat. He purloined his sorrow into a journalist's fury in Somalia, his indignant voice echoing across the French-speaking world. He was desperate to understand what had driven the Balkans to insanity, and why humanity had turned its back on Rwanda. He kept a suitcase packed. He never let up.

"I cannot rest in this small place," he'd said to her once. He'd just returned from Sarajevo. He had a deadline to meet.

"But I live here and I love you, and doesn't that matter?"

"Have you seen my disk?" He yanked open a drawer. The disk was loaded with war-crimes documentation. She'd retrieved it from the clutter of his desk.

"Would you put it in my laptop, please?"

Valerie did, but before she could zip the bag shut, he grabbed it and ran out the door.

* * *

Valerie became mute, overwhelmed by so much sorrow. When Gerard discussed human rights with his auspicious colleagues, she'd find reasons to be elsewhere. In recent years the burden of pain that entered the house had grown worse. She told her husband this. "Is it because you've forgotten that I love you?" he asked her.

Perhaps she had. Or perhaps he'd forgotten that she loved him. Often he was too preoccupied for sex. Yet she, too, had become absorbed in another kind of life.

* * *

Gerard was a Montrealer, but she'd met him in Toronto thirty-one summers ago. He'd been the superintendent of a stylish little brick-and-gabled rooming house, his father's investment, a place for a worried Quebecer to put his money, a hedge against the French province detaching itself from an English nation. In his spare time, Gerard had tended its garden with a skill Valerie admired. When they married and bought a home in Toronto's west end, she was still unused to short summers and the chill climate of Southern Ontario. She asked Gerard for some gardening tips.

"There's nothing special to know," he said. "The plants come with directions." He seemed indifferent. Yet he offered to dig the beds for her.

On a warm October Saturday, Gerard began to turn over the soil. With his foot on the edge of the shovel, he thrust his weight into the ground, heaving dirt out of the pit, forming a trench. He was city-bred, yet he had the dishevelled attractiveness of a farmer, his muscles conditioned and used to hard work, a casual ease in his body that she'd always loved.

Moments later the sunlight paled, crushed by a fist of cloud, shards of it falling upon a lean and shadowed figure in working clothes, a tired man who looked as if he were digging a grave.

"Gerard?" she said.

He didn't answer.

"Everything's okay, sweetie?"

Nothing. She felt certain that he couldn't hear her. *"Ça va bien?"*

He looked up, his face drawn. *"C'est fini maintenant.* I'm done."

Valerie planted bulbs and filled in the trench with soil. She became a skilled gardener. Years later, when the kids left home and Gerard became a freelance correspondent, she studied horticulture, bought a truck, and began to hoe and plant, water, and mulch for busy Torontonians who didn't have the time. Dark loam rich with life, a living bed of earthworms and microorganisms — through it she bound herself to all that gave substance to the living world. With a shovel, she'd turn the soil, get down on her hands and knees, and scoop up a clump or two. *Could use peat or bonemeal,* she'd think; *a bed of oak leaves for acid.* She had a good touch, a practiced sense of texture and weight. Up close she'd sniff the warm smell of decomposition, the microscopic nursery of all living things, and then time broke open in her hands, space dissolved, and the pliant soil became the ground of human habitation, the fields on which farmers toiled, and the dirt roads on which soldiers marched and terrified people ran. She began to feel in the earth the warmth of flesh, of Gerard and his cameraman dashing across Sniper Alley in Sarajevo, or bribing Syrian border guards with cigarettes and cash, or trailing refugees across dangerous frontiers in Eritrea. Then she met woe: the souls of women in Somalia and Rwanda, their bodies ravaged, their gardens soaked with blood. She didn't have to travel to find sorrow. It was the soil from which the world was made.

Long ago her husband dug this grave.

She didn't know how to tell Gerard that his grief had seeped into her bones. Nor did she know what human thing she could do about any of it.

In Saint-Pierre, she'd hoped to talk to cousin Marguerite about Gerard, to ponder her own life, to find words to say to her husband that would ease the burdens of intensity and silence. She worried that their marriage might be over, that whatever joy they'd known had disappeared. They didn't know how to talk, the two of them. Not to each other.

Valerie meandered up the slope of the town's streets as they turned northward and toward the hills. On Rue Maréchal Foch, tiny clapboard shops and restaurants were jammed together in crazy, irregular rows, as if some gravitational force were pulling them down the hill and into the sea. She kept walking upward.

3

SAINT-PIERRE HADN'T CHANGED much in thirty years. It had fog and salt air and the raw and blistered charm of an old fishing village. Now there were auto shops and a Home Hardware as well as *brasseries* and cafés. Salt and dampness peeled paint from weathered dories nudging the shore while in the centre of the old town, colour ran wild along the outsides of the squat frame houses and *pensions* — rich gold and deep green, flaming red and vivid pink, crimson and midnight blue. It was a tradition here, to paint with extravagant hues. Valerie thought of her pretty brick house in west-end Toronto, its trim beige shutters and door, its brass accents, its tidy lawn and garden. It seemed bland compared to this frayed wire of a place with its sparks of wild light, its gritty flashes of colour.

Gerard's cousin Marguerite and her husband Robert rented out rooms in their *pension* on a narrow street that sloped above the water. Behind it, they tended a large garden sheltered in a warm patch of sunlight. Robert had painted the house bright blue, its trim red. Its windows were lace-curtained and flush with the street, open to the glances of neighbours and pass-ers-by. When Valerie arrived a few days ago, she'd imagined people peering in the window, and the thought of unwelcome company made her anxious. Robert looked at her with a careful, appraising glance, as a sailor might ponder a bad sky.

Feel at home here, he said. *You are our only guest.* He took her bags upstairs.

Retired from the fishery, Robert looked older than his sixty-six years. His hair was white. His eyes had a clear blue sparkle rare in the island's sky, and his tanned face was creased like a map folded over and over along familiar lines of latitude and longitude. More than this, his detachment felt familiar, and as Valerie looked at him, she felt in his distant gaze the comfort of her father's presence. Had her dad lived, he would have looked at ease in flannels and baggy pants, his rod and tackle in hand. Perhaps she'd wandered into a land of ghosts.

You need a nap, she thought.

Or maybe her father was alive in this fisherman's body, gliding around the house in silence, his eyes on some distant horizon. Valerie looked at Robert again. She liked the man's reserve, or thought she did. Far away and here, all at once.

***

When Valerie showed up at the *pension*, Marguerite was resting her bandaged ankle on a stool. She'd fallen from a stepladder. Robert had been suffering from a bad back, just when there was much to do in the garden — completing the harvest and tidying the beds before the first frost. September was warm here, but island weather was unpredictable. Valerie assured Marguerite that she'd help.

"I am not dropping hints, *ma chère.* You are on vacation."

"It's all right."

Marguerite looked suspicious. She was a plump woman with coppery hair, her green eyes as alert as a hunter's. "You could have gone to New York with Gerard," she said.

"He's working."

"Or fooling around." Marguerite chuckled.

"That's not funny."

"Yes, I agree. When you said you were coming alone, I thought you were finally divorcing him."

How nice of Marguerite — barging into her roomful of troubles. Not even knocking.

"He invited me to come with him," said Valerie.

"So it is you who are out for adventure."

"Not exactly. Just time alone."

"I did not mean to be unkind," said Marguerite. "It is always so *sérieux* between you two. No play."

Valerie found it grating that Marguerite presumed to speak with such authority, having seen her cousins only at the occasional family party in Montreal. Yet Marguerite's emails were frequent, and they often hummed with flippant remarks — Valerie had forgotten that. Thinking to change the subject, she pulled out her photo album and flipped it open to a picture of Andre.

"My oldest," she said. "In Manhattan."

"He takes after you, *oui?*"

"Only in looks," said Valerie. She told Marguerite about his Internet business. He'd won an award for web design.

"He must be rich. Handsome, too. Has he got a girlfriend?"

Andre had a partner with hair the same bright copper red as Marguerite's. Her son had met James in Toronto when they were in college. James Eliot Wilson — she kept his card in her wallet. He'd been studying Culinary Arts when Andre fell in love with him.

"No," said Valerie. He didn't have a girlfriend.

Another photo showed her daughter, Chantal, who lived in Paris with her husband. She echoed Gerard's dark looks and easy smile. Marguerite seemed pensive as she gazed at her. She closed the album. "Your kids are far away," she said.

Valerie reminded Marguerite that her own two sons had long since left the island. One worked in Montreal, the other in Paris.

"You and Gerard also left home young," said Marguerite.

"Kids do."

"Only you settled down. Gerard is still leaving home."

"It's his job."

"It is too dangerous, what he does." Marguerite hoisted herself up, made her way to the sideboard, and found a decanter of brandy and two glasses. "You know about Ora," she said. "I think he does it in memory of her." She filled the glasses, and Valerie drank hers down at once. The burning sensation eased out words as if they were splinters under the skin.

"He still calls out to Ora in his sleep," said Valerie.

Marguerite put her hand over hers. "It was such a shock, her death."

"Over thirty years ago. It should have worn off by now."

"She booked a flight on the wrong plane, *ma chère*. No one gets over a tragedy like that."

Marguerite filled Valerie's glass again. She looked thoughtful as she gazed down at her plump hands. "You are still slim," she said.

"It's my job. All the digging."

"Years ago Ora gave me a gift I can no longer wear."

Valerie swigged down the rest of her brandy.

* * *

She'd known about the bracelet for a long time. It had been Gerard's gift to Ora, and he'd learned only after her death that she'd given it away. It happened that during spring break, the two young people had taken off for Saint-Pierre while Gerard's parents were wintering in Florida. There was no sane reason for this chilly escape (as if Montreal winters weren't cold enough). Ora lived with an open-minded aunt who didn't mind if Gerard spent the night. *We wanted adventure, and I'd never been to France*, he said. *Ora had only been to*

Paris. He made it sound as if his sweetheart had missed out on the real France.

It was 1970. Marguerite loved the Beatles, and Gerard brought her the *Abbey Road* album to thank her for hosting them. Yet it was Ora who gave her the gift she treasured. Ora had left behind her bracelet, and Marguerite was about to mail it back when she received a telegram telling her to keep it as a token of appreciation. Two weeks later, Ora was dead.

She must have sensed she was going to die, said Valerie. With sadness, Gerard agreed. *Love is a thing you give away,* he said. *That's how it is.*

* * *

When Valerie went to her room, she found a velvet jeweller's box on her bureau. The bracelet sat inside it, a polished silver oval adorned with a delicate filigree design and held shut with a thin chain and a clasp. Valerie put it on, admiring its cool beauty. She wondered how Gerard would react to the sight of it, if he'd grab her wrist and cover it with kisses. *Poor man.* The bracelet was just as likely to cause him pain.

Inside the velvet box was a photo of Ora. Valerie gazed at the young woman, her expression of sixties dreaminess, her long, glistening hair upswept. She'd seen that same look on her own face long ago, so full of hopeful yearning. There was bravery and fearlessness in being young, a thing she saw in her children and heard in herself only as faint music, like an old song on a radio with poor reception. *Bravery. What Gerard loved.* She gazed at Ora, her elbow resting on a table, one hand cupping her chin, her bracelet gleaming.

Valerie took the picture and tucked it into the mirror frame. Glancing at herself, she began to brush her long hair with vigorous strokes until it began to ripple with light. Then she swept up her hair and styled it, glancing at the picture, pinning her thick coils into the same twists and waves. Effortless, all of it. Her touch lighter than air.

* * *

In the dark of the following morning, Valerie dreamt that Gerard's hair had turned white. *He's grown old too soon,* she thought, and then a loud *bang* startled her awake. It was the front door opening and closing — Robert returning from the *pâtisserie*, and then she remembered where she was. Wanting to get an early start, she put the memory of the dream aside, got up and made the bed, soothed by the cheer of its blue and white quilt, by the crisp white paint of the iron bedstead against deep blue walls, by the lace-curtained windows overlooking the park and the water. It had style, this decorative warmth — crisp and pressed with a certain fastidiousness she'd come to think of as very French. She dressed and put on the bracelet. Her thoughts stumbled. *Gerard and Ora. They slept in this room.* Yet so had she and Gerard. The glint of silver didn't erase that.

Today was Marguerite's sixty-fifth birthday. Her sister Lisette had invited the three of them for a late evening meal. Only her *petite soirée* was going to be a surprise party with a guest list of a dozen. It mystified Valerie that Lisette had managed to keep it secret. Neighbours in Saint-Pierre weren't shy about dropping in for tea or, in the case of the local gendarmes, a shot of brandy. There was lots of talk. There couldn't be too many secrets here.

On the night table, Valerie had left a list of household tasks. She'd bake a *tarte aux pommes* for the party. *Yes, I took the butter out of the fridge.* Gerard would have chided her for being so fastidious. *You see what's wrong with us,* he'd say. *A workaholic married to a drudge. For this you gave up a trip to New York.* Only Gerard was no better. He was on a working trip, and he wouldn't relax into Big-Apple fluff and razzmatazz. It was instinctive, that in his favourite noodle shop on Mott Street, he'd check for rat droppings. If he found them, he'd go to City Hall and report it. It must be something genetic, she mused — this lopsided attention to detail. "All this way you've come to do my housework," Marguerite chuckled, but Valerie had asked her to treat her helpfulness as a birthday gift. Today she shouldn't have to work, especially with an injured ankle.

In truth, Valerie had fled here. She'd had no idea what she'd do in the wild isolation of Saint-Pierre. Something was unravelling in her that only simple work could knit back together. Perhaps she was too anxious. These days, she didn't sleep much.

When she went downstairs, she found a plate of fresh croissants waiting in the kitchen, along with a pot of strong black coffee. *I should thank Robert,* she thought. In the sitting room, she heard the TV, a newscaster reading headlines. Nothing much, from the sound of it.

Robert looked up, as if to agree. *Rien de nouveau,* he shrugged.

4

T HE CLOCKS' RACKET BEGAN to fade as Valerie strode up
the steep hill and out toward the city limits of Saint-Pierre.
As she walked, she could hear those mechanical noises melting into the shape of a voice. It was soft and urgent, almost a
whisper in her ear.

As for me, I am about to change direction.

Before email, Matt Reilly's letters came in pen and ink. By
the time the first one arrived, Valerie had married Gerard.
Matt's notes were tucked into Christmas cards which he'd
begun to send the Lefèvres after his stint in Vietnam. Each
December for the past twenty-five years, he'd mailed them a
holiday greeting from Boston, a card illustrated with an elegant
Renaissance nativity or a gold-embossed Latin inscription
or the square notes of Gregorian chant; each wishing her
and her family the blessings of the season. The note would
mention — and sometimes accompany — his latest book.
A prayer card enclosed with his first mailing showed a host
and chalice on one side, and the date of his ordination to the
priesthood on the other.

"*Merde*," said Gerard. "First he kills people, and now he's
a priest."

"He was a lost soul," said Valerie.

"A clever soul. He'd better not write about you."

"Why would he?"

"Who knows? Like Saint Augustine with his mistress and child, and then he finds God and writes a bestseller."

"That's enough."

Gerard apologized.

Matthew's first note had been abject, assuring her that she'd been right to break up with him, that she'd married a man far better than himself. By then, five years of marriage and two kids had brought happiness. *Matt must find it lonely at Christmas,* she'd said to Gerard. He didn't reply.

Valerie always waited until after New Year's to answer his holiday letter. Over Christmas, she'd read just enough of his new book to respond to his gift with thanks. His titles suited the whims of each decade: *Love: The Ultimate High* or, in a recent, more reflective mode, *The Wide Web of Grace.* It was pastoral psychology, popular work that struck her as insipid, but he had a Ph.D. in the subject and there was an audience for what he wrote.

A few Christmases ago, an email address had come with Matthew's card. *I've found your gardening website, and it feels like Eden before sin,* he wrote. Valerie went online and told Matt to pitch the holy water and talk like a normal human being.

I shut myself out of Eden once, he wrote. *I'm not so sure that I'm a "normal human being."*

So you're a Martian, she answered. *Just don't wallow in your lousy past.*

She'd said a great deal more than that, and he wrote back. *Thank you for your frankness,* he said. *It has been years since anyone has been so direct with me. You have done me a great kindness.*

She continued to write to him when Gerard went to cover the war in Rwanda. Every evening she'd email Matt, choosing careful words to tell him that she'd married a man still troubled by the violence he'd witnessed as a youth in Quebec.

When Gerard was home, his need to talk about politics was compulsive. Knowing he was suffering, she'd warm him with kindness, as if he were fevered and chilled from the lack of it. She'd put whisky in his tea. She'd light a fire.

She began to pick through his copies of *Foreign Affairs;* she'd read the news online in French and English. Although she could engage Gerard in conversation, it didn't seem to matter to him. He travelled more often than not. She wondered if he'd been unfaithful on these trips. Sometimes in bed, he was as full of passion as a young man, but sometimes he turned his back to her. Yet with the passing of time, she desired him more, not less. She decided not to look further, to love him as he was.

In writing to Matthew, Valerie's comments were spare. Domestic life was off-limits. She never talked about her children, never mentioned their names or ages or accomplishments. With equal discretion, he emailed his solace and encouragement, more a psychologist's words than a friend's. He raised the subject of male infidelity as a weariness of soul, and when she didn't respond, he chose to address her suffering by telling her about his life as a priest, his struggles with loneliness, the comforts he'd found in philosophy and religion. They'd talk online, at a safe distance. It was, at least, a conversation.

Two weeks ago, he'd emailed to tell her that he wanted to leave the priesthood. He'd compared it to moving from a room to an apartment, from ascetic pleasures to aesthetic ones. After the trauma of Vietnam, the narrow confines of his vocation had given him time to mend a tattered life through prayer and work. He'd suffered unspeakable loss in the war. No, worse than that.

She didn't want to remember what he'd told her.

God knows I had it on my conscience, he'd written earlier.

So did everyone, she thought. Meaning the war.

Matt, she suspected, meant more than that.

He now felt that remaining a priest would only encourage a fear of life in its richness. Exhausted from too many obligations, he was about to take a rest, to visit his sister in Los Angeles. *In a month I'll be in Toronto,* he wrote. *Would you like to join me for dinner?*

She'd declined. She was afraid she'd end up in bed with the loneliest man on the planet.

In truth she still loved Gerard, in the same deep, inexplicable way that the soil loves light. It was in the hope of pondering all of this that she'd come alone to so barren a place.

* * *

Gerard had held her in tenderness, walked with her in trouble and worry, and she could feel him as an amputee might feel a ghost limb in its absence. Striding upwards, into the hills above Saint-Pierre, she imagined walking with her husband in Manhattan, navigating the narrow, downtown streets running east off Lower Broadway — Pearl, Water, Beekman, Maiden Lane. Streets rolling down the eastward slope of the island, snagged on bedrock and unravelling like a ball of wool in a cat's paws, all the crooked charm of the old Dutch town tumbling into the South Street Seaport and the East River. Gerard was with his cameraman, checking out shoots of the Brooklyn Bridge for later in the day when the sun would be behind them, a nice backgrounder for the opening of the Quebec fête at the waterfront pavilion. Less than two kilometres west of him, Andre was asleep in his loft in Soho, exhausted after a workaholic's twelve-hour day with a handful of corporate clients. James, off for job training at a rooftop restaurant, would have tiptoed out by now, eager to master the details of cooking breakfast *en haut*. He would have closed the door with practiced silence, his hand on the doorknob turned clockwise, the door shut with care, the latch engaged by the slow counter-clockwise turn of his hand. Valerie had seen him do this once, and the studied gestures intrigued her. His silent and careful hand on the door seemed to show a thoughtfulness that was also a fear of being observed.

As James walked his early morning block to the E train at Spring Street, heading down the stairs, swiping his card in the turnstile, the subway doors were opening on her daughter Chantal, stepping out at the Métro Franklin Roosevelt in Paris. The Canadian Embassy was a few metres away from her stop — a nice job in the cultural office that let her out at mid-afternoon to lunch with artists visiting from Montreal and Toronto. That evening Chantal would have dinner with Valerie's sister, her Aunt Karen, who'd been in London for a scientific meeting, and who'd fly into Paris this afternoon.

Morning and evening of the third day in Saint Pierre — one simultaneous moment stretched like plastic wrap across six time zones, the world too elusive for something as flimsy as time to seal in place. Matthew was in Boston, setting his watch three hours back to Pacific Daylight Time, on his way to visit his sister on the coast. He was headed for Logan to catch his flight, his cab stuck in rush hour traffic.

Don't bet on it, she thought. In his holiday letters, Matt had joked about ruining book tours by missing his flights. Something would come up, some church thing. Now and again he'd leave earlier than planned, before anyone figured out excuses to detain him.

* * *

Valerie was beginning to feel dizzy. Thinking like this had done it, distorting the world into one continuous moment, bending the fabric of space out of shape so that she was here and not here, too. Across the road was a park square, benches, and a fluttering tricolour. Valerie paused to watch four older gentlemen in berets playing *pétanque* on the other side of the square, tossing the silvery balls around. She drank some water. The dizziness passed.

It was damp for late summer, the island muffled in fog. Something felt amiss, as if she'd imagined not only the moment that held her family, but also the apparition of an *horlogerie* and its racket of clocks, the sight of the old men playing their game, the scraps of cloud enveloping her. Imagination was continuous and unfolding, like a bolt of cloth — and just as real. The truth was that everything you looked at had to pass through the lens of what you imagined you saw. It was up to you to decide what was real.

5

THESE WEREN'T HIGH MOUNTAINS on Saint-Pierre, nothing above three hundred metres. Steep, grassy slopes folded into valleys, and the hillsides were lush with green and studded with rocks for footholds. Valerie made her way with care. As she advanced toward the highest crest, she could see a gauze-white dusting of flowers against the green slope. Upward she climbed until at last she found a cluster of rocks sturdy enough to bear her weight. Then she crouched down to get a better look. Close to the ground, below the tatters of fog, she could see for herself the bone-cold frailty of everything that lived here. She wasn't sure what this tiny flower was — she'd never seen it before. In her jacket pocket was a guidebook of *fleurs sauvages*, and she pulled it out, flipping through the pages. *Diapensia lapponica*, that was it. Five-petalled flowers nestled in thick, matted green, the tough leaves hugging the rocky soil, the plant groping for a roothold. She examined the slight blooms and their sturdy leaves, noticing how well adapted they were to the damp chill and the wind.

Remembering her moment of dizziness in the park, she got back up on her knees with care. From her backpack she pulled out her camera and photographed the flowers. She wanted to make notes and there was nowhere to sit. Her map told her that she'd walked north toward a pond called *Pain du Sucre*, Sugar Loaf, then eastward and up into the hills above the coast, meandering along a twisting path beside trees stunted by wind and clumps of shrubbery that hugged the face of the island. She could see the waters of L'Anse Coudreville in the distance and the shore road leading into town.

The fog began to lift, the sturdy hillside shrubbery glittering in the light, the blue sky unfurling like an enormous flag. Fog-bound most of the time, the island was brimming with sky. Valerie felt uneasy, as if the sun were a brassy intruder. She remembered her first summer in Canada, vacationing with Matt just before he left for Vietnam. They were walking in a farmer's field near Tottenham, off the Airport Road, twilight hovering over the blue sky, when they saw a huge fireball streaking across the western horizon, gold with a hue of green; magnesium, he told her. *A meteor. Make a wish,* he said, but she felt sad for this decomposing chunk of matter that might have once belonged to a lost civilization, and she didn't want to wish upon this poor rock's fiery misfortune. *Meteors happen,* said Matthew. *At least they go out in a blaze of light.*

Glancing again at the brilliant sky, she felt the same uneasiness, as if the sun had emerged from the curtain of fog to take a bow before the play ended, before earth's star collapsed into a coal-black dwarf, knocking out the planet's delicate balance of gravity and angular momentum. Moments from now, the earth would wobble off its axis, topple over, turn into a snowball, fall and never stop falling. She grimaced. *That's your marriage you're worrying about.* Or maybe not. Maybe she'd taken a wrong turn, meandering down the cul-de-sac at the end of time. She heard no birds, no rustling of trees in the wind. No wind.

* * *

Valerie noticed a sheltered grotto in the rock. Sitting down on a flat stone, she pulled out her notebook and began to sketch the flower parts of *diapensia lapponica*. As she looked at this slight little bloom, she remembered reciting a poem for Matt, one of Tennyson's. *Flower in the crannied wall/I pluck you out of the crannies/I hold you here, root and all, in my hand....* She tried to remember what came next ... *root and all, and all in all....* The rhythmic words seeped into her body, along with the sun on the warm rocks. She closed her eyes.

In her dream, she's climbing the slope, in no particular hurry. Not climbing; drifting because she can't feel the ground. She's a wraith. She can move as slowly or as quickly as she wishes; she isn't bound by time or distance or impeded by obstacles in her path, and just as she begins to wonder if she's dead or alive, she feels a rushing sensation, and she's no longer walking but flying. Overcoming gravity, she knows she's alive. Only Ora's inside her, and the longer she flies, the faster she flies, and with speed she experiences the weight of her mortal body. Higher and faster, a human meteor about to burn up in the atmosphere, a red-hot torch that sets the blue cloth of the sky on fire, and it's only now that she understands that the ancient firmament is made of glass, that the sky itself is a curtain rent from top to bottom, that she's about to fall and will keep falling until the hard rock of earth slams into her. The last things she sees are the meadow flowers racing up, an enormous whiteness.

* * *

Awake, Valerie remembered Ora's presence in the dream and she felt afraid. She looked at her watch. She'd been asleep for fifteen minutes, but nightmares were friends with darkness, with three a.m. in a frightened child's bedroom. She'd woken up to daylight as brilliant as the dream itself. Maybe she wasn't awake yet.

Below and to the east, she saw the wet and sinuous curve of the shore road snaking toward water, the cove jammed with picturesque dories and fishing boats bristling with radar. There were squat fishermen's cottages clinging to the sides of hills. She thought of mudslides and erosion dragging these frail batches of timber into the sea, and she wondered why she hadn't seen the danger before. Yet the boats and the houses, solid and real, reassured her. There were no clouds in the blue sky, and the sun was beginning to roll southward. It was almost nine-twenty, and she'd had enough for this morning.

Valerie started downhill, wending her way along the narrow, overgrown paths, gripping tree branches, stumbling on rocks. It was a three-kilometre hike from here to the edge of town, and once she'd made it to the bottom of the hill, she kept an eye out for the park where she'd rested earlier that morning. There it was, near Rue Maréchal Foch. The old men playing *pétanque* had gone, but she noticed a set of silvery balls rolling around in the square, as if the game had ceased only moments ago. Or was continuing, played by ghosts.

※ ※ ※

Downhill she walked on Rue Maréchal Foch, edging along the narrow sidewalk past ramshackle shops, past houses lit with colour, each with its lace-curtained window, each curtain stitched with white-on-white patterns of windmills and sail-boats, each windowsill holding its tangle of potted geraniums in flower. Silence. Mid-morning and no traffic, no gridlock of mini-cars and vans, no honking klaxons and irritated drivers. A short block away, she saw the photo shop on a side street, and she looked for the *horlogerie* next door. It was gone. The fog had wrapped itself around it and fled. Time had folded it up and put it in its pocket. Valerie felt uneasy.

She walked through town along the shore road. The water was calm with a glassy stillness, and she imagined a bright river lapping against the pier, Gerard standing just below the

Brooklyn Bridge, feeling the power of its cabled steel, an enormous loom weaving everything into its play of light. He and his cameraman were ambling along, walking up Wall Street to Broadway, standing beside the Morgan Bank, its concrete wall nicked by an anarchist's bullets. *That happened back in the twenties,* she recalled, *and they never caught the guy.*

In the centre of Saint-Pierre, the promenade was empty, along with the benches surrounding the fountain at Place du Général de Gaulle. No customers sat at the café tables; no young mothers were wheeling strollers and chatting. As she passed the *gendarmerie,* she saw a police car whizzing off in the direction of the airport. Past the harbour she walked; past the *quais* where the ferries left for Miquelon and Newfoundland. Nothing was moving. It reminded her of the game of Freeze they used to play as kids — everything held in suspension, like human chunks of fruit in aspic. It felt like the East Coast blackout of the sixties. Her mother's stove off. Her neighbour's lights out. Then the whole street dark, the shoreline dark, an entire city of blackness. City after city after city.

A bomb that kills people, but leaves buildings intact — what's it called? She couldn't remember. She still felt exhausted from the time-change, not to mention the hike. Prone to misjudgement, to the mind playing tricks — even on vacation, she was overdoing it and losing sleep. *Ten-forty a.m. Two hours ahead of Gerard.* Strange, how she measured time, as if New York City sat on the Prime Meridian. Here she stood in a tiny speck of France where everyone took it easy at mid-morning. When she got to the *pension,* she'd take a nap.

She glanced again at the water, imagining a boat, a ferry, a water-taxi plying the East River. Gerard was smiling because he loved the water. Now he was facing the river, eyeing the reflective surface of a building, wondering how to work that bouncing, morse-code light into a news clip. He'd leave Henri to fiddle with the light meter. *Rue Amiral Mueslier*. Before her was a bright blue house, trimmed in red; a sign out front: *Pension Gervais*. Robert's black Pugeot was parked on the street. Valerie walked up the stairs, turned the key in the lock, and opened the door.

* * *

She stood in the hallway. To her right was the dining room that led into the kitchen. To the left was the living room, its sunny front window crowded with geraniums, the lace curtains pulled wide open, the furniture protected with plastic slipcovers from the bright sheet of light. The room had the formality of an old-fashioned parlour, the sort of place where no one sat but guests who came for dinner. Down the hall, at the back of the house, was a TV room. Part of the room had been a porch once, but Robert closed it in, leaving the back door that opened on to the *potager*, its produce ready for harvest. Last night Marguerite was saying that the vines were heavy with ripening tomatoes, that they had to start picking them for canning, and here she was with a twisted ankle. Valerie had told her she'd look after it. *Is that the TV?* She listened. It was.

Injured or not, it wasn't like either of them to be indoors on a fine day.

Valerie walked into the TV room. From where she was standing, she couldn't see what was on the screen, only its pale, unnatural glow reflected in the fixed stares of Robert and Marguerite. Beyond them, the back door was open, a bright square of daylight punched into the shadowed room. It framed a patch of garden, staked vines bending under the pendulous weight of ripe squash, enormous leaves, brilliant yellow flowers.

Neither Robert nor Marguerite turned to look at her.

"Regarde le télé," Robert whispered.

Look.

II.

6

A BLUE METAL SKY, gripped by a pair of giant bar magnets. In the split second before she understood what was wrong, Valerie heard Gerard's voice and saw a picture that was not on the screen. *Comme les aimants*, he'd said of the Twin Towers, and she'd laughed. The words for *magnets* and *lovers* are close in French. They'd been visiting New York, the four of them, riding the Staten Island ferry. *Mama, what's so funny?* her son asked. Andre was six, Chantal, four, and she repeated his question, because she always repeated what Andre said.

Robert's voice cut in. *Un avion a écrasé,* he said. A plane went right through the building. One of the towers was dark with smoke.

Then Valerie saw what everyone else saw.

Marguerite's son was on the phone from Montreal. He'd just seen it, live on TV.

When Valerie was young, she'd seen a plane disappear into the sky. It never returned. *Maybe it just did.* The thought prickled the back of her neck.

Gerard's watching this, too. She imagined him eyeing the glass-fronted buildings along the East River, his cameraman ready to shoot when the sky broke into a metallic shriek behind them, the sounds of an immense iron fist crushing through concrete and steel. In the building's reflective glass, he'd see fire.

He'd turn around.

* * *

Her reactions were too slow, as if time itself were turning into a thick and gelatinous substance, like the waves of Lake Ontario in winter. Yet in spite of this, her thoughts quickened, awash in a flood, sluices bursting open, sounds pouring into her, and perhaps she was only imagining that the barrier of her physical self had dissolved, that in the heat of fire, her soul was melting into every other soul. *Help me*, someone yelled. *Stay calm,* said a woman on the phone. *Help is on the way. Break a window. Take a damp towel, roll it up, cover the base of the door.* A man's voice was shaking. *The earth is the Lord's, a psalm of David's.* He began to recite, knowing he was about to die.

"How many people work there?" asked Marguerite.

Valerie didn't know.

"They say fifty thousand in the towers," said Robert.

Space had collapsed, like that blue tent of a sky. And with it, distance. *Chantal! Andre! Gerard!*

She thought of everything, and all at once.

Life is a struck match, lit by grace. All it is. All it ever was. Time is over.

* * *

The TV voices faded. In the screams and cacophony of fire, there was the sound of a rescuer's voice, her sister's. *Look, Valerie. Look.*

She was falling away and downward into memory, into a green shimmer, a golden luminescence, a girl of ten peering into the eyepiece of her sister's microscope. *Cy-to-plas-m,* Karen sounds it out. *The round blobs are chlorophyll,* she says. *They swim in it.*

Cyto— ?

—Plasm. It's — basic.

Valerie wonders what she's looking at.

Pond grass epidermis, says Karen. *One cell thick.*

Karen's seventeen, her sleek, dark hair in a page-boy, her glasses off, her vision deep enough to see the invisible parts of life without the aid of an instrument. She's wearing a pink sweater-set, a grey skirt, loafers and knee-socks, and she's about to take part in the Science Fair at Groves Island High — the only girl who's entered the exhibit. Valerie looks again, imagining that she sees through the eyepiece a line of emerald chloroplasts afloat in a river of gold, but the gold fades as the green grows into a formless blur in her field of vision, a green pond of light sorting itself into the fine detail of duckweed and bracken. She imagines pond grass, clumps of it at the water's edge, cattails protruding from their fronds.

When she was little, Karen would tell her that if you put a cattail in water overnight, you'd have a kitten in the morning. Valerie was mad when it didn't happen. Now she's ten, picturing these tall brown spikes near the water, looking hard into the eyepiece as if she might find them, if she were about to see something wondrous, a soft form that'll scamper across the rocks, wet and hungry.

A dark shape, that's what her mind's eye conjures up, but nothing she'd ever seen before, nothing feline, nothing to do with the grasses. A huge brown-coated object, floating face down.

She pulls away.

What's the matter? asks Karen.

Nothing, says Valerie, but she doesn't want to look anymore.

Later, she tells herself. She stops remembering and glances up at Marguerite's TV. There are too many dead as it is.

* * *

"Gerard, where is he?" asked Marguerite. Her eyes were afraid.

Valerie felt too stunned to answer.

"In what part of New York City?" Marguerite picked up the telephone and dumped it in her lap.

Valerie dialled. *Answer, answer.* Her mind began to close the circuit. *Please be alive for me, Gerard.* She'd forgotten Andre's number. *Gerard, you know it.* Ringing, ringing. *There's no one here to take your call right now.* The sun was gleaming on the table's edge, its wood-framed glass cleaned and polished by Marguerite's attentive hands. Gerard was working. Her husband didn't like to be disturbed at work. She must have written Andre's number down somewhere.

Gérard, je regardais le télé, I was watching TV, she said to his voice-mail. *Quel catastrophe.* She left him Marguerite's number. She asked him for Andre's. What a terrible feeling, she thought, to be so far away from a loved one who could be in danger. Worse was to realize how in the frantic thumping of her heart, his heart was beating, too. Yet it was possible that Gerard had no idea that this disaster was being televised, that even the residents of these remote islands were watching the fire with horror and dread.

It was one of those moments, thought Valerie, when the heart sees everything at once. She grew up in New York City, yet whatever remained of that distant past was flying apart, as if the plane had struck her. She needed to know where Gerard was.

On répond? whispered Marguerite, her eyes full of worry. She stared at the phone.

Pas encore, Valerie answered. *Not yet.*

She hung up. *I hope he doesn't have a silly ring-tone,* she thought. Like *"The Yellow Rose of Texas."* She started to giggle.

"What is so funny?"

"Gerard and I have been married all these years, and I don't even know what his ring-tone is."

Marguerite looked at her with consternation. She offered her chamomile *tisane* to soothe her nerves.

Valerie's ring-tone was Beethoven's "Für Elise," a song her mother loved to play. *Come and sit with me,* she'd say, and she'd pat the piano bench. She introduced her daughter to Tchaikowsky and Mozart, and Valerie learned to hum their melodies, even if she wasn't that interested in piano. Only the tunes had been mangled and crushed into ring-tones, hundreds of chirpy ditties all going off at once, and at that moment, the jangle of "Für Elise" was spilling out of someone else's cell phone, yanking some poor guy away from his coffee and laptop, and he heard his wife crying that a plane crashed a few floors below her and how much she loves him, and Valerie's hand was shaking as she tried the phone again. Only now there was no getting through to New York.

"We'll have to wait," she said, to no one in particular.

Marguerite set the tea tray down. "Does he have an email address?"

As if he'd be checking it right about now. "We'll have a line soon."

Robert was staring at the TV. *"Les pompiers sont arrivés,"* he said, as if the firefighters were parked outside.

Valerie slumped over, face in her hands.

Her mother's playing the piano. From nowhere, the sound of it comes, the consolation of Mozart and Brahms. This was how the woman dealt with sorrow, with the sight of her husband sitting in his armchair, sipping rye, falling asleep, his soft snoring like a deep bass instrument playing its own tune. *Your dad's tired,* her mother'd say. He worked downtown, in the office of the Medical Examiner. *If he were alive this morning,* thought Valerie, *he'd have lots to do.* A quiet and methodical man, his drinking was as careful as his lab work. When he'd nod off, her mother would stop playing the piano, go to him, take the glass from his hands, help him to bed.

He wasn't belligerent. He was as still as a parched tree absorbing rain. Only her mother got fed up and stopped playing for him until the evening when he came home with a gift for her, a white silk Chinese dress, patterned with lavender wisteria. *Are you going to try it on?* asked Karen. Their mother was a slight woman with straight black hair, and the slender style suited her. She returned to the piano, wearing her pretty dress and a look of resignation. Her husband's eyes were bright. He filled his glass.

* * *

Valerie called Karen in London. "Have you spoken to Gerard?" her sister asked.

"I can't get through."

"You will, honey. Wait a bit."

The words embraced her. She's four years old and her big sister's patting her head, saying *be a good girl* — but she's fretful, as children are who won't be consoled. Karen's promising to push her on the swing, to walk with her through the zoo and point out the animals. The zoo was close to the Bronx River. Dark and sinuous, slithering over the rocks below, a serpent in the grass that river was.

Valerie dried her eyes and glanced at the TV. *There's no way out,* she thought. *When the world starts to break, you break, too.*

"What are you seeing on the news?" she asked her sister.

"The same thing you are." Karen paused. "Over here, there's speculation."

"How do you mean?"

"That it might have been deliberate."

"Who would have done such a thing?"

"The world is full of crazy people, sis," she said.

Valerie tried to pretend she was wrong. Her sister had such empathy with the living world. When they were kids, butter-flies would rest in her hair like flowers. Chickadees would feed from her hands. Life felt safe around her. She was just repeating something she'd heard.

* * *

Valerie's father liked to fish the Bronx River. A photo shows him wearing an old cap, flannels, a vest and dungarees, his tackle and bait in hand. He was a tall man with dusty hair and blue eyes, a veteran of World War Two, one who appears awkward, uncertain if he wants the camera's attention. You sense he's trying to hide the fact that his eyes see more than they should. Worse is the feeling that if you look into his eyes, you'll see his mind unravelling. He doesn't smile. *He lost all his friends in the war,* said Valerie's mother. The Japanese captured him in the Philippines, but he escaped. His friends did not.

Valerie realized that she'd never thought too hard about her father. Now she couldn't avoid these facts. They were punching their way through the new idea that the crash might have been deliberate. On TV, the screen exploded in a roiling fireball, a bloated, disgusting spectacle, a rotten orange showering its garbage all over Lower Manhattan. Her mother used to say that no one wanted to know how their father had suffered. These were the folks who went and saw war films instead. A commentator viewing this plane crash said *it's just like a movie.* Her mother would have answered by saying *how vulgar. A plane hits a building, and this is how you entertain yourselves.* Only Valerie found it hard to take her eyes off the screen. If Karen was right — if it wasn't accidental — this loop would run in everyone's head forever.

Pray she's wrong.

"When did the plane crash?" she asked Robert.

"Just before you came in."

His face darkened as he stared at the TV, his voice hushed, his eyes on the burning tower. It was the fault, he said, of too many planes zigzagging across an overcrowded sky, of buildings many times taller than they should be. Sooner or later, he insisted, an accident was bound to happen.

Marguerite scowled at her husband. *C'étaient les kamikazes,* she said.

Valerie's dad had a buddy named Mr. Troiano who'd served in the Pacific during World War Two. The boys in her class said he'd been on an aircraft carrier that had been sideswiped by a kamikaze pilot who'd missed his target and plunged into the sea. *The fighter passed right in front of his nose,* said Matthew. *Mr. T. could of pissed on the Rising Sun.* Maybe that explained the hidden castle where the vet found safety, because nothing else could explain the huge key-ring swinging from his belt, the clinking and jangling sounds of the keys as he strode by. Tall and muscular, with thick, black hair — everyone thought he was a giant, like Bluebeard. In fact he was an engineer with the New York City Department of Public Works, and he carried the keys that opened and shut the intake and outtake valves at City Hall. He knew all about water mains, about pipes in danger of bursting. *Can you go shut the tower valves, Mr. T.?* Valerie could hear the clanking of his keys, the thud of his hard boots on concrete. He could fix the whole damn thing. Sure, he could.

Mr. Troiano scowled at talk of kamikaze planes, and she felt sure that her father would have done the same. Her mother said that whenever he remembered the war, her dad would grab his fishing tackle and leave the house. At this time of year, he'd fish in the lake and wetlands of Van Cortlandt Park, in the Pelham Bay lagoon, and on Twin Island to the east. He'd cast off from shore, or he'd rent a rowboat, exploring ponds and inlets and marshlands. She didn't know that he ever caught much beyond the look of wild apparition that he carried home in his eyes. It seemed to his daughter that in the seclusion of a wooded inlet, he must have had visions. The souls of the faithful departed drifting among the trees and rivers; it was possible.

Everyone in heaven is a saint, said the sisters. *Does that include soldiers who died in the war?* asked a classmate who'd lost his dad. *Yes,* sister answered. *You can pray to your father.* Valerie's dad knew a lot of men who'd died, some of them Catholics, his Irish fishing buddies from before the war. Only he'd stopped going to church. *God understands,* said her mother, when Valerie inquired after his soul. He fished alone.

* * *

The boat overturned, his body face down in the water. He'd been drinking, said the police.

Until moments ago, Valerie had never conjured up this scene, had never wanted to see it. Only she knew that time had been upended, that she couldn't escape what had happened. *Regarde le télé,* says Robert. *Look, Valerie.* Look into the depth of greenery, says Karen. Cherish the plant with its one-cell layer of thickness, its emerald chloroplasts. Look at the dark stain shadowing the water — look at her father who drowned in search of his friends, look at time collapsing in fire and ash, his lost buddies crying out from the tower windows. Look at the flame at the tip of the match. Cup your hand against the gust of wind that takes it all away.

7

Trying to use the phone, Valerie couldn't even feel it in her hand. She'd become a conduit of senseless information, as if she were a chopper pilot hovering above the burning tower. *Ch-ch-ch-ch*, rotors slicing air. Transmitting and receiving, the world pressed to her ear.

The phone rang. "Hello?"

Silence.

Gerard. I know you're there. "Is that you, Gerard?"

Calm down, she thought. *This phone must be on the blink.* The island's dampness could rot the wires. Gerard would try her cell.

Marguerite was in the kitchen when the phone rang a second time. She picked up the extension. The voice on the other end was loud enough for Valerie to hear.

"Happy birthday, *ma chère*." It was Marguerite's sister, Lisette.

"*Merci.* It is a birthday like no other."

"But I have sad news."

"We haven't had enough?"

"Laurent Sarazin died last night."

Valerie didn't know this man. She listened. The telephone made Lisette's voice sound hollow and tinny. Monsieur Sarazin had had a massive stroke. "The poor man," the woman kept repeating. Her thin voice crackled with shock.

"I know, I know, *ma pauvre*," said Marguerite. *"C'est terrible."*

Lisette wanted to speak to Valerie. She picked up the phone and expressed her condolences.

"Merci," said Lisette. "Marguerite doesn't know that the Sarazins were supposed to come tonight."

"He'll be missed, *oui?*"

"By everyone. He owned the *horlogerie*."

Valerie remembered the name on the plaque by the door.

"Could you bring an extra tablecloth?" asked Lisette.

"Oui. Of course."

"Bien. On my lunch break, I'll buy the flowers."

What if Gerard's trying to get through? thought Valerie. *Or Andre?* She told Lisette she had to go, and why.

"Don't worry, *ma chère*. The media make too much of things."

Valerie hung up.

* * *

Nothing in this world happens without consequence, she thought. She would have imagined that in the middle of a worldwide news event, the fate of Laurent Sarazin would resemble the tree that falls in the forest with no one to hear it. Yet it wasn't so — not at all. In Marguerite's telling, the man was a good neighbour, and therefore it was no small thing that he'd died. Had he been a tree, he wouldn't have had a thudding fall. Yet the town would have mourned the lost shade of his flowering branches, their reliable production of sturdy, chill-resistant leaves. A native of Saint-Pierre, the owner of the *horlogerie* wasn't a clockmaker or an ingenious inventor, or even an obsessive tinkerer as Matthew's dad had been. His accomplishment was to have sold everyone in town a watch or an alarm clock. He'd kept the *saint-pierrais* on time for work and school, for soccer matches and christenings. He'd made the rambling flow of days a little more coherent.

She saw Robert standing by the back door, his head bowed. His skin looked raw, as if lashed by rain. His hands were clenched together.

"They were buddies," said Marguerite, her voice soft. "From school days."

"Why don't I leave you two alone," said Valerie.

"He's already gone."

Gone where?

Robert unclenched his hands, gazing into the far distance. Invisible was the ocean, his hand on the rudder, a sail leaning into a bitter wind.

* * *

Lisette had tied up the line for only a few minutes, but Marguerite checked her voice-mail anyway. Nothing. It felt to Valerie as if a dark star had blocked out all transmissions, had made it impossible to reach her loved ones. No matter how close she imagined them to be — New York City was at least in this hemisphere — her family's light was reaching her eyes from the great distance of a lost time. She could only look back at them, as she would at starlight. It was beginning to feel ridiculous, that she'd try to call her family.

"Who called before Lisette?" asked Marguerite.

"I think it was Gerard."

Marguerite looked puzzled. "You *think*?"

"I didn't hear a word."

"Then how could you know?"

"It was the silence," said Valerie. "That's how."

Marguerite looked skeptical. She put a hand on Valerie's forehead. A moment later, she was pointing at the TV, as a plane veered into a steep bank, and a second tower disappeared in the smoke.

"*Maudits kamikazes!*" she yelled.

Gerard! Valerie grabbed the telephone and started punching in numbers.

She listened. No answer, not even his voice-mail.

It felt to Valerie as if some mighty law of nature had failed them. In that case, there'd be no one to blame for magnetic poles destroyed, the earth in a dizzy wobble, the wild swinging of gyrocompass needles that sent planes swerving off course and crashing into buildings.

The newscast noted that both of those planes had flown out of Boston. As Matt might have done.

Her mind groped for an explanation. She thought of the plane that had vanished into air when she and Karen were children. Maybe it had just returned, transformed into an angry hornet driving its needle-nose into the tower. Soon would come another lost plane, and another. Fighter-bombers, kamikazes from World War Two, single-engine Pipers and Cessnas, the plane that carried Gerard's beloved Ora, all of them hurtling over the edge of time. Only time is an arrow that points in one direction. You cannot come back.

And I'm nuts, she thought.

Where are you, Andre? And James?

Valerie held the receiver to her ear, and strangers' voices roared in her blood. *We're as high as heaven. The plane crashed below us. Please help.*

Putting the phone down, she rifled through her purse, looking for James's business card. She found it, turned it over. Andre's number was scribbled on the back. She grabbed the phone again. The line was dead.

"I can't get through to my son," she said.

"*Ma chère*, you haven't dialled," said Marguerite.

She tried Andre's cell and got a recording. *Please try again later.*

Marguerite turned up the sound on the TV. The newscaster said it was a terrorist attack. Two planes had been hijacked, and the culprits were from the Middle East.

Gerard used to talk about these guys, thought Valerie. *I should have paid more attention.*

Robert left the kitchen and went upstairs.

Valerie felt dazed. "I'll have to phone again," she said.

"*Ma pauvre.*" Marguerite patted her arm. "Later. It is all right."

* * *

Dank waters of memory rising, her father drifting away, Robert setting out to sea, and Valerie herself was far from home. She could feel sun in the warmth of Marguerite's touch, in the brilliant colours of the garden, in the morning when the sky collapsed on Laurent Sarazin. *What madness.* She imagined Madame Sarazin, paralyzed with shock when she learned what had happened. She'd know the woman by her stricken look, the same as her mother's when the police came to the door.

The phone rang again.

"Tell them my birthday is cancelled," said Marguerite.

It was Valerie's daughter, Chantal, calling from Paris.

"Thank God, *maman,* that you're not in New York," she said.

"Maybe I should have gone."

"Have you spoken to Papa and Andre?"

She had to tell her daughter, no.

Chantal started to cry. The sound startled Valerie, as if moments ago her young daughter had fallen off her bike, as if she'd need stitches.

"*Maman,* have you ever lived through anything this terrible?"

No, said Valerie, she had not.

Yet as a child, she'd lived through a deep sadness, one belonging to the same downtown that was now under siege. She couldn't tell her daughter that sometimes life flips a switch and the past lights up, as if it weren't the past at all but some part of the present hidden in shadows.

Years ago, the shops on Canal Street had bright red banners with Chinese characters for good luck and prosperity, but her family, still grieving for her father, didn't notice. Her mother's hand felt brittle, and her Aunt Ann was saying, *Now Valerie, you're the birthday girl, and what would you like?* because Karen had already chosen a yellow paper parasol with a green pattern of leaves. Valerie wanted her father. She wanted the ache in her heart to go away.

She'd felt bewildered by all of it — painted fans, joss sticks, embroidered silks, her mother picking through a rack of Chinese dresses. Valerie wanted to hold on to her so she wouldn't go away, too, so she ran over and hugged her mother who didn't respond, who kept pushing aside each flower-patterned dress, the hangers squeaking against the metal rack, her face streaked with tears, crying in front of such a pretty display, and then Valerie was crying, too. Karen put her arm around her sister. *But it's your birthday,* she whispered. She dried Valerie's eyes with her handkerchief, then drew her under the parasol. *Be good,* she said. *I'll help you choose a gift.*

"You will let me know when you hear from *papa*?"

Valerie told her daughter that she would.

After she hung up, she turned on the kitchen TV. Another plane had been seized, or maybe two, or maybe more. No one seemed to know how many. *You're safe, you're not in America, be glad you've come to an isolated place,* she thought. Yet she worried about going outside, as if some *avion détourné* might fall through the broken sky above the island, as if a rockslide of lost souls would rumble down and crush her.

Valerie's thoughts went skidding off the road. *They're with God,* said her mother. *Now* and *then* collided until Valerie didn't know which was which. The police had closed off Canal Street and New York City was under martial law. Her mother was weeping for the dead. Her Aunt Ann wanted to treat them to Chinese tea and sweets, but Canal Street was black with smoke, and all the shops were closed.

Valerie didn't know why anyone would be eating.

In the middle of an attack.

8

S HE REMEMBERED OTHER TRAGEDIES, other acts of violence, life under martial law. Valerie and Gerard were newlyweds in the autumn of 1970, living in Montreal when terrorists kidnapped a British diplomat and murdered a cabinet minister in Quebec. *There is no excuse for this,* said Gerard, his face contorted with disgust. *They should throw those* cochons *in jail.* Every morning, he'd read the news, then toss the paper in the garbage.

"Has Chantal spoken to Gerard?" asked Marguerite.

Valerie glanced at the newspaper on the kitchen counter. Nothing in it made sense now.

"Valerie?"

"I'm sorry?"

Marguerite picked up the newspaper and tossed it in the recycle bin. She repeated her question.

"No," said Valerie. "Chantal hasn't heard from him."

I want to hear your voice, Gerard. And yours, Andre.

"Do you like *soupe aux artichauts?*"

"Of course." Valerie was puzzled by the question. "Only you can't do any cooking on that ankle."

"Don't tell me what I can do. I can sit on a barstool and cook, if I like. How about *charcuterie?* A glass of wine?"

What if Andre were on the phone, glancing out of his office window. A black roar's slicing through his life, breaking win-

51

dows and smashing computers. Everything stinks of carburant. Every paper's burning. Cochons.

"You'll feel better, *ma chère*. A little food," said Marguerite. *Power out; a stairwell full of smoke.* Valerie wasn't hungry. She'd never imagined Andre in business. He used to be unfocused but then he met James, and then he figured out how to make money, and now he stacks up his early-morning appointments like a busboy balancing a tray-load of dishes, never breaking one. *What a kid.*

All my best corporate clients are in the towers, said Andre. *Every day, I'm in there.*

He'd told his mother that, he'd said it more than once, but she had a blind spot around Andre. She never got his facts right. She'd formed this bad habit of sifting his remarks through her mind like heavy soil through a fine screen, saving his rich observations, discarding the mundane. When he told her where he worked, she'd kept imagining some skyscraper in midtown Manhattan, that big one at Lex and Fifty-something with the sloping glass roof. Those twin downtown towers had seemed too remote, somehow.

* * *

If only Andre were here for lunch, thought Valerie.

He'd love Marguerite. It's the food. He fell in love with James over food. James used to dish out advice and snacks to classmates weighted down with deadlines. *There's a formula to writing an essay,* he told Andre when they first met. *First have a slice of banana-hazelnut bread, you'll need the energy. That's called Breakfast 101. Now use the intro to describe what you're doing. Then use the ending to describe what you did. That's two pages right there. Have some more bread. Fresh coffee.*

All food is communion, he said later. *Not those dried-up things they dish out in church.*

James would come to the Lefèvres for dinner, bringing aged Boursin, a bottle of Pinot Noir, and a fine-grained bread he'd baked that afternoon. He'd cross himself and say grace and he'd cut the bread, pour the wine, and raise a glass to toast the family's kindness.

"I just don't get the 'hang' of James," said Gerard. "He is so *religieux* and—"

"He wants to live a moral life," Valerie replied. "That's what Andre says."

"But going to church?"

"Imagine your parents throwing you out of the house," she said.

"That wouldn't send me off to church."

"Me neither. But my aunt used to say that if no one understood you, God would."

"You think James had an aunt who said that?"

"Maybe."

* * *

James had emailed her about his new job in the tower restaurant. *So high up, you can see God,* he'd written. *And Andre, if I had binoculars.*

Robert came into the room, his sailor's face still ravaged. He eyed the TV news, then Valerie.

"Don't be afraid," he said.

"I worry that my son is in that building."

"Your son's young, with two good legs," he said. "He'll run."

Andre would run nowhere unless James were safe, she thought.

9

J AMES HAD TOLD VALERIE that he wanted to be a chef, that he hoped to open his own restaurant. She'd taught him how to make *tarte aux pommes*. Taking the subway downtown this morning, he would have been imagining lightness — eggs in cloudlike pastry, *crêpes* made of air. *I'll put your* tarte *on my menu one day*, he'd said.

Valerie glanced at her watch and counted back two hours. In New York City, it was ten past nine in the morning.

She had to keep busy. Keep trying the phone.

She'd left the butter out overnight. The dough for the *tarte* had to be made ahead, then chilled. In the cupboard were dry ingredients for baking. A bowl of crisp red apples sat on the counter, ready to be washed. She surveyed everything in the kitchen, walking with care like a hospital patient hooked up to time and its steady drip of news, forced to make a ponderous moment of each second because that was the only way she could absorb things. *A rope and ladder, my ordinary life.*

* * *

When you bake, said Gerard, *you look like a Flemish woman in one of Rembrandt's paintings. You hold that particular light of day. That silence.*

At this moment, she held nothing. She was a dust-mote sifting through light. *All of us are dust,* she thought. There

54

was no point trying to make sense of things. On the kitchen counter, between the bins of sugar and flour, was a mini-TV, full to the brim with bad news, with commentators trying to sort things out, to fit this mayhem into some structure, into a story with a coherent plot. *What a joke,* she thought. In her hands she could feel the hum of life, and she understood that the day's good work would strengthen her. She turned the TV's sound off.

Her spirit went looking for Andre, rifling through her messy closet of a life in search of some comparison to this tragedy, something she already understood. *Doesn't this remind you of the time when...?* Images drifted before her eyes. *It's a bit like this*, said memory. *Try this.*

She thought of her childhood, and the plane that disappeared.

Only this catastrophe wasn't like that.

It wasn't like anything at all.

* * *

When Andre was sixteen, Valerie took him to Groves Island, her childhood home a few kilometres north of the city boundary. There she'd gazed out over Long Island Sound from a ragtag cluster of old frame houses, their front steps peeling paint and creaking underfoot. Andre said, *It's* old *here, Mom,* and she said, *New York City's old, too.*

New York's a different kind of "old," he replied.

Everything changes in different ways, she'd said to him. *Everything flows, nothing abides* — those were the words of a Greek philosopher whose name had slipped her mind. When she was a child, she'd lived in the north end of New York City, in the Riverdale section of the Bronx. Aunt Ann and Uncle Joe were Groves Island people, and her aunt and mother were sisters. After her father's death, Valerie's family moved to the island to be close to their relatives.

Life changed for her, but the island began to change, too. Valerie told Andre how it used to house an army base, and how its main street, once nooked and crannied with bars and honky-tonks, now played host to chaste and pretty coffee shops, organic greengrocers, fitness clubs. Her childhood home remained the same. Their mother had kept up the old wood-frame cottage with the screened-in porch, a family gathering-place entangled with wildflowers and haunted by their youth. The house was Karen's now.

Some things grow older and younger at the same time, Valerie told her son. *Like a scabby old bulb that puts out a green shoot every year.*

Like New York, he replied.

After their visit, Valerie and Andre returned to Toronto, and her son grew into a young man who longed to live in his mother's hometown. He was a restless kid, always running late for class, taking the stairs two at a time. *Like a herd of elephants,* his father used to say. *Slow down.*

Greased lightning, said Andre.

He did business in the South Tower, eighty flights up.

Mom, I work out. Don't panic.

Her thoughts were melting in the heat of fright.

* * *

The phone rang. It was Gerard. His voice was a gale-force wind that howled through her body. Valerie had to sit down.

"You're all right?" she asked.

"I am safe," he said. "It is horrible—"

"Have you spoken to Andre?"

"Yes." He paused. "He tried to call you, but—"

"Where is he?"

"On his way out of the building. I am off to find him."

"*Sois prudent,*" she said. "Be careful."

"It is madness, total disorder. The authorities—"

"Give Andre my love."

"That son of ours, I'll give him a kick in the pants. I had to yell at him to leave the building."

"Because of James?"

"No one knows where James is. Please don't ask me."

His voice was strained, like the sound a branch makes, creaking under the weight of ice.

"I'm here," she said. "It's okay."

Gerard cleared his throat. "Try to imagine," he began.

* * *

Gerard had his back to the tower as it exploded into flames and he saw its shattered reflection in the building glass up ahead. Merde, *he yelled, and looking behind him at the darkening cloud of smoke and ash, the spiral of computer paper, spreadsheets, email printouts, he felt certain that whatever had happened was no accident. He and his cameraman ran down the slope of Wall Street, through the crowds of men and women trying to escape along the zigzag of side streets to the north and south. Gerard was heading in the direction of the river, to South Street, then northward to the pier. He knew Manhattan. He knew that there was an escape route by sea, that it was too dangerous to run back up Wall Street to Broadway. On the pier he found a water taxi, and he told the driver that they were Canadian journalists. He asked the driver to take them downriver a kilometre or so, then into the bay, drifting south of State Street and the Battery.*

Up ahead, Gerard could see the skyline of Lower Manhattan, the fiery wound in the North Tower. It was almost nine a.m. Eastern Daylight Time and he was already on the phone to Montreal. He told them about the crash, and they patched him into the morning radio show. They were going live to air. Gerard started to talk. Only he wasn't sure what he was talking about, or if his words were making sense.

Time was unspooling from its reel. He spoke for hours, or seconds.

Then he remembered his son.

* * *

While he was doing his live report, he witnessed the second plane crash. He described what he saw, but someone else was talking — a calm, dispassionate man, not Andre's father. Moments after he hung up, his cell rang.

"Hello, Dad?"

Pale as a seashell, Gerard gripped the deck rail.

"Andre, are you all right?"

"They took the hit a few floors below, but there's a stairwell open."

"You get the hell out of that building."

"James is trapped next door. I told him—"

"Bout de crisse, never mind what you told him. Move your fucking ass. Right now."

* * *

"You used to yell," said Valerie, "when he took the stairs two at a time."

"He always did the opposite of what I said. God knows—"

"Don't be afraid. He's got a head on his shoulders."

"I'm not afraid, *chère* Valerie. Just angry."

10

ARGUERITE'S CROCKERY BOWL was dun-coloured, pressed with a pattern of flowers and leaves. With a spatula, Valerie began to scrape the softened butter out of its wrapper, but Gerard's anguish was shivering inside her and the butter almost missed the bowl because the spatula was shaking in her hand. Moments later she knocked over the canister, spilling the sugar on the counter. She grabbed a tissue, dried her eyes, cleaned up the mess, and started measuring again. *An easy recipe. I've made it dozens of times.* She turned on the electric mixer, watching the beaters spin into a blur, blending the ingredients into a smooth, buttery paste. *Butter and sugar,* she said, as if she'd never seen them before. *Flour's next,* but never in the course of history had someone chosen to fly a plane into a skyscraper, and she had to remember to measure the baking powder into the flour without knowing where on earth her son was. She turned off the mixer, took the spatula and scraped the paste from the sides of the bowl.

Time flipped over inside her, fierce and blue, cloudless at the island airport where her Uncle Joe tuned up Cessnas and Beeches and the single-engine Piper belonging to Mr. Groves, a descendant of the island's founding family, a decorated hero of World War Two. There was a crowd, lemonade, and ice cream, a stand bedecked in red, white, and blue. Mr. Groves hadn't flown since his combat days. Valerie and her family were in the crowd of well-wishers who saw his plane take off for a spin, its propeller humming, and then the little girl watched it disappear into a soft pleat in the sky's fabric, the day's blue curtain drawing shut around it.

Valerie asked her big sister what she'd seen. *Just the angle of reflected light off the wings,* Karen said, *creating an optical illusion.*

She didn't believe it.

He'll come back, said her sister.

He didn't.

In a moment of terror, Valerie understood that Mr. Groves was never coming back. Worse than that. If a grown man could vanish into the sky, then she herself would never again be safe. She'd become wraithlike, a sheer curtain through which all breezes would pass, including a howling wind of indignity, her Gerard.

See for yourself, he'd say to his TV audience. *There are people who are going to die, up above where the plane hit.*

How vulnerable they both were. His skin, like hers, was as porous as air, the lost souls on those airplanes drifting through his body, his nerves crackling with their voices. *Please help me, I can't breathe,* and the 911 operator's voice, *It's okay, honey, help is on the way.*

Looking for his son, Gerard would be as enraged by injustice as he'd ever been. *This isn't good enough. They should send a fleet of helicopters to rescue those above the fire,* because he knew that James was up there, too. He could hear the *ch-ch-ch* of the police chopper overhead, his bones wired to pick up messages.

All those voices singing through his nerves would have told him that this was the way of the living, the fate of humankind. How often he'd said it to her, that the day starts in innocence and at the end of it, the innocent are always dead — if not by some gunman's hand, then by disease or starvation or accidental stupidity in the wealthiest city on the planet.

That, she realized, was what his admirers liked about him — his knife-edge of honesty. It was something she admired, also.

He'd believed her that she once saw a plane disappear.

* * *

She measured the flour because the blue sky was malevolent. It was as good a reason as any for filling the scoop, for weighing its contents on the scale. *Three hundred fifteen grams.* Perhaps it made her feel calmer — knowing that even this weird causality was sane, compared to whatever reasoning let someone crash a plane into a building.

What's happening? she asked herself. *What's going on in this world?* She made her living as a gardener. All she knew about were flowers. Her botany textbook taught her the facts. There were reasons why things happened. Flowers bloomed because of light, water, minerals in the soil, pollinating bees. *It all comes together rather well,* said her prof. An amusing guy with a gentle sense of humour, he pointed out that nothing was simple. Plants were made up of water, minerals, proteins, chlorophyll, and so on — but if you broke down all of these into their chemical components, if you watched them interact, you might find out that the chain of causality went on forever, that everything causes everything.

A lot of good that does me, Valerie thought.

Godawful things just happen.

When days and years returned to their normal order — if they ever did — she would say the same thing of this moment, of her native city and its suffering. *It just happened.* Gerard would explain the politics, but nothing more. Before her eyes, a single fire blazed and it was endless. Doused in one place, it flared up in another. War there, terror here. If you remove the grid of time, it is all one fire.

11

IT CALMED VALERIE to imagine James beside her. *Here, let me show you how I make this crust.* She'd taught him to use semi-soft butter, and he'd objected, and she knew why. In cooking school he'd been told to use chilled butter for pastry, *but listen,* she said. *Once you've made the dough you'll have to chill it anyway, so what's the diff?*

"So show me how you roll it," he replied. "How you get it from the board to the dish."

"And then you have to try, okay?"

When his turn came, he made a mess of it. He looked chagrined.

"Nobody gets it right the first time," said Valerie. "Or the second and third."

"In class they'd call you an Easy Mark."

"Just patch up the rips in the shell. Once you fill it up with fruit, who'll notice?"

"You have a good heart," he said.

* * *

She kept working and she imagined Andre sampling the *tarte,* but having spoken to Gerard, Valerie felt her eyes tearing up, her lungs about to fill with smoke. She could still feel her husband's desperation, his fear crackling in the air. *Stay low to the ground and stay where you are,* said the 911 dispatcher to some frantic caller, said the slight breeze coming through the window, said everyone on earth with ears to hear. *Watch yourself.*

On va mourir, she thought. *They're going to die.* She wiped the flour off her hands, then turned the TV off. Not watching didn't help.

We can't breathe, we're going to suffocate, we're up above where the plane hit, the smoke is rising.

Valerie could feel James beside her as she worked.

You have a good heart.

Putting his foot through a window, desperate for air.

12

ON MARGUERITE'S WINDOWSILL was a jar of lavender cuttings. Valerie touched a soft handful of silver-grey leaves and tiny purple flowers. Their fragrance drew her back into the everyday world, the one in which, whatever else happened, she'd have to live out her days.

Her mother had taught her to bake. *One-eighth teaspoon of baking powder,* she'd say. Only Valerie was in France, a country of decimals, not fractions. *Point-five millilitres,* the spoon read. Karen had once tried to teach her metric measures. *Give it a try,* said her sister. *It's not as hard as it looks.*

Alone now, Valerie measured with care. She felt helpless.

While her mother gave piano lessons, she'd practise baking, stirring her mother's lavender into the batter, along with a sprinkling of Brahms and Mozart. *What does this recipe call for? One egg.* Cracking it on the side of the bowl — what pleasure it still gave her, a smart flick of the wrist that broke the shell, the yolk slithering into the mix, round and gold as the sun that warms the skin, even when the skin is chilled with dread.

Taking the spatula, Valerie folded in the flour and baking powder. Thanks to her mother, she'd come to believe that the world was full of unheard music. She'd taste its richness in her baking, feel the hum of it in flowers, in rocks, in the dew on the grass until the silence ended on a summer night with her Uncle Joe in the backyard strumming his guitar, looking like a Mexican *gaucho* with thick black hair and a moustache. He was playing *Malagueña* and Valerie switched on, all five senses whirring. She could taste the sharp *ping* of starlight, feel the music plucking at her body. She learned guitar and began to sing.

By the time Valerie could strum a tune, she was thirteen, and she knew her neighbour Matthew.

"You're learning to play *git*-tar," he said to her. "Like Elvis."

She tried to do that lopsided Elvis smile.

"Maybe Andrés Segovia," she replied.

Matthew's silence was as deep as a well. "You'll have to play for me," he said.

"Do you like music?"

Matthew nudged some gravel and dirt with the toe of his shoe. "Don't know," he replied. He lowered his eyes, as if he'd said a shameful thing.

* * *

She sang and played him a folksong called "I Gave My Love a Cherry." It had beautiful words.

A story when it's telling, it has no end.

For sure, that lyric was true. She'd once seen her own heart on a medical technician's screen, that tough little fist-sized pump, the rhythm section of her body. *How long's it been doing that,* she wondered, unable to imagine a beginning, not believing that at a specific moment, someone in the Heart Department had thrown the switch that triggered the *lub-dub, lub-dub* of a few tiny valves in her chest. As she'd gazed at the screen, she felt she was witnessing an elemental rhythm, one that had infused her unborn self, one that had no end. Her heartbeat wasn't hers alone.

It was Andre's, too.

* * *

All of fifteen, and you were sitting on the hallway stairs, hunched over into the music of my old guitar, plucking out chords and a melody. Your strong tenor singing went soft and low, the way a young voice gets when it's shy with poetry, lost in a tune still spinning through the mind, so I knew you must be composing a song and I said to you I had no idea you even played, *and you said* a little *or* no big deal, *as if words might end the magic, as if music were your beloved and the two of you needed time alone.*

You knew we were a musical bunch. You'd met your grand-mother and your great-uncle Joe. You knew, of course, that I played guitar. It's like I'm trapped, *you'd joke.* Inside a musi-cal-family dynamic.

You and J.S. Bach, *I replied.*

You thought life was unfair, that Gerard and I had grown up in the sixties, that we'd had the best pop music ever written. How you loved plucking out those old Beatles songs, gentle ones like "Michelle" and "Norwegian Wood," but you'd smile as you played your own songs, your singing so soft that I never did hear the words. You'd slip back inside yourself, strumming the guitar, doing runs, your hands forming the same chords my hands had formed, inventing the same rhythms.

* * *

What a kid. Valerie put the pastry dough into the fridge. She thought of her family's love of music, then of Matt who now preferred Gregorian chants and the masses of Bach and Mo-zart. He'd said once that many inspired compositions were based on folksongs. How odd it was that years ago he'd been slow to react, unsure what to make of her when she started to play guitar.

"But now he *loves* music," she said out loud.

She didn't notice Marguerite leaning against the doorway, tapping the side of her head.

"*Mon Dieu.* Who are you talking to this time, who isn't here?"

Valerie was embarrassed. "A friend of mine who's flying today."

"No, your friend is not. No one is."

He's not flying into New York, she thought. *He's fine.*

*   *   *

She could see him striding toward the boarding gate, tall and lanky as prairie grass, the glint of sun in his hair, his grip on a scholar's briefcase full of papers, his blue eyes dreaming awake. As if he were still coming home from Vietnam, still consoled by his call to the priesthood. She wondered if Marguerite could read her mind. She felt sick.

"*Pauvre* Valerie, are you all right?" asked Marguerite.

Maybe Matt flew yesterday.

"I've felt better," she replied.

She didn't want to get more specific. Marguerite might think she had a lover.

Her stomach began to settle down. She didn't welcome the thought of throwing up, even if a plane came down and hit the island. Her mind felt jammed full of planes tumbling out of the sky. She decided to imagine Matthew whole and well.

Marguerite had something in her hand, a wad of mail.

"Birthday cards," she remarked. "From my youthful neighbours."

"You have lots of friends."

"*Oui,* and imagine, we'd thought of flying to Paris. To celebrate with my son."

"My sister's flying to Paris today."

"From what planet, *ma chère?*"

"Planet London."

"I hope she brought along her Walkman," said Marguerite. "She is flying nowhere."

* * *

Valerie tidied up, feeling rueful as she rinsed off the baking implements. She'd heard that those madmen who flew into the towers had used knives to hijack the planes. She put knives in the dishwasher every day, but there was no refuge in domestic arts, no world apart from the world. For the rest of her life she'd knead blood into bread. She thought of her garden, its rich soil a grave.

Even so, there was work to do. There was a special knife to slice those apples. She glanced at Marguerite's butcher block. One slot was empty; the bread knife was lying on the counter. Valerie rinsed it, dried it, put it back in the block. *Maudits kamikazes.* She scrubbed the bowl, fists clenched like a fighter's.

13

WHILE SHE WORKED, Valerie imagined Matt alive, remembering how they were young together, the boy who'd lived at the end of her street. His property faced on Willow Drive, an old brown-shingled stump of a house set deep in its wooded grove, its back to hers. From what her family could see of it, untidy oaks and sycamores shadowed the yard and the house was hidden because the path to the back door was overgrown.

Matt was an only child with few friends, except for a sallow-looking kid with wiry hair the colour of rusty fenders, a pest who got As in everything, as well as suspensions for setting off cherry bombs in the schoolyard. The two boys spent lots of time together, but Matt's buddy had a slingshot, and once when Valerie went down the slide at recess, he aimed it at her and she ducked, but he hit her anyway. Matt was standing right there, and he didn't try to stop that creep. *Scaredy-cat Matt*, she'd thought. Her mother was furious. She bawled out the kid's parents, and Matt's, too. Sister made that smart-aleck apologize in front of the class. After that, he left her alone.

Still she'd wondered why Matt had just stood there.

She was about twelve years old at the time, and soon afterwards she saw Matt sitting on his stoop, working a piece of wood with a knife. Curls of wood fell away from the blade and what emerged was winged and delicate, like a chick wriggling out of a shell. He noticed her, then lowered his eyes.

"That's neat," she said.

"My dad taught me. He learned from an army buddy."

"Can I hold it?"

Matt handed her the bird. "Our dads were in the army together," he told her.

She didn't know how to answer.

"My dad died," she said.

Matt fiddled with his knife. "Bet he was a hero," he replied.

She told him he was. When she went to give him back his bird, he wouldn't take it.

"You keep that," he said.

Valerie thanked him.

"I'm sorry about what happened. I should've beat him up."

She was pleased and worried at the same time. Then she heard it: *tick-tock-bong, tickely-tock-bong.*

"What's that?"

"My dad's clocks."

"How come they're so noisy?"

"He makes them himself. That's how come."

Valerie recalled that she'd never liked the sounds of those clocks, but she was impressed by the fact that Matt's dad had made them. Summer found her hanging out in his backyard. The murmur of the clocks enticed her — the tickety-rattle of minutes and seconds, all talking at the same time. After a while it seemed that the din shaped itself into the low whisper of secrets, and she could feel them humming in her ear, as if they might tell her something if she'd listen.

* * *

Valerie had Matt's cell phone number, but when she tried, she couldn't get a connection. She realized she had no idea what time his flight would have left Boston. He might still be in the taxi — tipping the driver, striding into the check-in at Logan Airport, its lower concourse a knotted jumble of cops, armed guards, frightened passengers. Ticket in hand, he'd glance at his watch, go talk to a cop, find out that all flights had been cancelled. Up the escalator he'd go, to sit in the café, to try absorbing the murmured news that a plane had struck a tower in New York City. He'd be horrified.

Then she imagined a croupier, shuffling time. New game. Cut and deal.

Deuces are wild. *What a gorgeous morning,* says the deuce.

This time, Matt's running to the departure gate, and he glimpses the sky, frail and blue as a robin's egg. He dashes through the passageway. As he boards the plane, he can hear the ticking of his father's clocks, the whole earth striking the hour.

14

MARGUERITE WAS ARRANGING her birthday cards on the dining room mantel. "You spoke to Gerard?" she asked.

Valerie told her what he'd said about Andre and his trapped friend.

Marguerite looked sad. "Your son will be one of the fortunate ones."

How do you know that?

She put the cards down and turned to face Valerie. "The TV says those trapped higher up *sautent par les fenêtres*."

She didn't even try it in English.

Jumping out of the windows.

* * *

Andre might help others escape down the stairwell. James was in the building opposite his.

"*So high up...*"

No. *James wouldn't fall like that. He wouldn't break like a clay pot. He wouldn't die today.*

When James died, he'd evaporate like beeswax, like the candles on the altar at mass. A lit substance melting into air.

She felt Marguerite's arm around her.

"The trapped man, was he someone you knew?"

"Know."

"I should not have mentioned what I heard. *Je suis desolée.*"

James would dissolve into light.

Time and space are a mystery. Valerie had seen Mr. Groves' plane as it melted into the sky. Except for Matt (and later, Gerard), no one had believed her.

The plane was never found.

Maybe it's still in flight, she thought.

James, too.

* * *

The years dissolved. She was only nine, standing in front of the newsstand on Washington Street, staring at a copy of *The Island Banner* with a photo of Mr. Groves' Piper Cub taking off from the island airport. Because she was a child with a good imagination, she saw the plane vanish a second time — first the nose, then the fuselage, then the wings and tail fading, and she broke out in a cold sweat, walked away from that headline as fast as she could. It was disappearance that terrified her. She remembered her big red ball blinking like a sightless eye as it rolled into the storm sewer at the curb on Willow Road, and how she ran home upset, wanting it back, certain that if something so large and bright could fall through that opening and vanish, then so could she. One day she'd step off the curb, her foot in front of the small dark archway in the stone, and gravity would reach up and grab her by the ankles. Down she'd go.

This was worse.

She'd pushed her way into Charlie Reilly's store, its screen door banging behind her. Victory Home Supplies, full of bric-a-brac. It was calm in there. Matt's dad, Charlie, was at his work-bench, buffing some tarnished silver. He waved hello.

* * *

"Would you like me to shut the window?" asked Marguerite.

Valerie didn't realize she was shivering. *As you pass through time,* she thought, *the temperature drops.*

"I'm going to water the plants," she said.

* * *

"You might say my dad was ahead of his time," said Matt once.

Valerie thought this was a bad pun.

Yet even as a nine-year-old, she'd known there must have been a reason why Charlie Reilly had given up his clock-making trade for commerce in useless junk. Unlike other businesses, his shop felt like a refuge, and he didn't mind little kids wandering around and touching stuff they'd never buy. Stained-glass table lamps, cathedral radios, painted chinaware from the Melba Theatre giveaways in the Bronx, trays jammed with cameos and brooches, crystal beads and silver lockets — memories tangled up in each other, poignant with the weight of years. Along with more than a few grinding, wheezing, tickety clocks, not one keeping time with another, all of them telling time as we know it on earth, although Mr. Reilly believed that we'd run out of time, in the true sense of that expression.

He looked up at her. "Something wrong, honey?"

She shook her head, no.

Of course there was something wrong. He was a war vet. He knew there was something wrong.

* * *

According to Matt, no one ever realized that the junk shop was Charlie's hideout, that the real Charlie had disappeared.

Valerie felt certain that Andre would vanish if he lost James. Fluent in French, he'd melt away into Paris or Nice, where the two of them had vacationed. He'd abandon his name, his profession, his driver's license, his email address. He'd have to rediscover who he was.

* * *

Or else, Andre, you'd be like water, cupped in James' hands, warmed by them. You'd become gaseous, invisible, floating away into air.

You'd be one of the lucky ones.

* * *

Eyes shut, she steps inside Charlie Reilly's shop which is still open, which will stay open until the end of time, where there are piles of abandoned cell phones ringing woe, along with the echo of a front door jangling, of ghostly shoppers coming in to buy trinkets or to bring in broken castoffs. All rivers run to the same sea. The old world has vanished, only to come crashing down again, and she imagines Andre and James and Mr. Groves and the poor secretary who wore some precious bauble to work in the tower this morning, the bride who touched her wedding ring as the plane took off. Mr. Reilly would have welcomed their business. He could refurbish anything, although he didn't believe in clocks anymore. He worked alone.

The world was running crazy, on Charlie Reilly's time.

Andre could learn the clockmaker's trade.

He, too, could hide.

15

NOT LONG AGO, Andre had taken a liking to plants. *Try African violets,* Valerie told him. *Or geraniums. You don't have to water them often.* She filled the watering pail in the kitchen, then made her way to the front room where she started picking off dead blooms, pouring tepid water into dry soil. Lemon-scented geraniums — their fragrance clung to the withered leaves crushed in her hand. *Blessed plant,* her mother would say of all its leaves and flowers, living and dead.

Those poor souls so high up — she imagined firefighters hurrying to rescue them. Uncle Joe's buddy used to work the fire-boats for the city, but most of the old tugs were gone now. There had to be a few left, in good enough shape to hose the buildings down. On Groves Island years ago, they'd put out a terrible fire, the worst in the island's memory. *I can't keep thinking about this. What beautiful leaves.* She touched the geranium's fresh, new growth, budding and soft.

James is patient. He'll wait for help.

Robert came into the front room. "I hear you have spoken to Gerard," he said.

"*Oui.*"

"And he has spoken to Andre."

Robert looked grieved enough. She could sense that he was trying to steer himself home from the shock of losing his best friend. It didn't seem fair that he'd have to drift into such a treacherous storm as hers. "You must keep trying," he said.

There were no lines open. Everyone in New York City was trying to call the police. Gerard reached me because he has some kind of dedicated line patched in through Montreal. All Andre had was his dinky little cell. Trust me.

Only it was she who had no trust.

Sautent par les fenêtres.

"Gerard told him to get out of there," she said.

"Oui. Bien sûr."

In Robert's eyes, she saw his grief for Laurent Sarazin and the echo of her father's anguish. She knew that if she continued looking at the man before her, she'd see her dad's lost buddies, a long line of starving men, off to Bataan in the Philippines, on a forced march to death.

"I'm sorry about your friend," she said to him.

"Merci," he replied. "I have known him all my life."

"This morning I walked past the *horlogerie.*"

Robert smiled a little. "Marguerite bought me a watch from his shop."

He held out his arm to show her. It was an elaborate wrist-watch, full of dials with hands and tiny numbers: seconds, minutes, hours; moon phases and time zones; dates, months and years. She imagined it might also include tides and temperature. She thought it must be a seaman's watch.

"It is that," said Robert.

Valerie admired it. She thought of Matthew's father.

"I used to know a clockmaker," she said.

16

∞∞∞

IT WAS ONLY BECAUSE of Matthew, because she used to practice guitar on his back stoop, that she knew Charlie Reilly. Not him, but his clocks, how they'd make the air ripple with odd and lonesome thoughts, fears and worries that got tangled up in her songs, and their wild, crazy ticking was almost a kind of music. They made her think about people who'd died, people who got lost. She'd have to stop and talk about them before she could go on playing.

"Do you ever wonder about Mr. Groves' plane?" she asked Matt once.

"What about it?"

"What happened. Where it went."

"Forget it. It's gone."

"I can't forget it. There was a thing in the paper. It's coming up to five years."

"What do they say?"

"'Rumours persist.' That he took off and disappeared."

Matt scratched his head. "Got that part right."

"What do you mean?"

"Could have changed his name. Maybe ran off with someone. His wartime sweetheart in France, or something."

"They don't say that."

"Not in *The Island Banner*. The family would sue."

She'd always believed what she read in the paper, and because the reporter wasn't more specific, she'd felt uneasy. Mr. Groves' plane might have passed through the barrier of time. Those were the rumours. Although no one could prove them, no one ever denied them, either. Maybe this could happen to anyone — and did, every day. Time was full of cubbyholes and stuck drawers. History was *old*. Mr. Groves could be trapped in some other era, somewhere very bizarre.

"You mean like the Pleistocene," said Matt.

"Something like that."

"Wonder how you'd get out of there."

"What bothers me," Valerie said, "is how a plane could just — disappear."

* * *

"'All that is solid melts into air,'" said Matt. "'All that is holy is profaned.'"

"Glad you think so."

Matt showed her the underlined sentences in *The Communist Manifesto* by Karl Marx. He wasn't a Marxist. He was reading it for history class.

"A cool way of putting it," he said.

"Anyway, it's just a story, that Mr. Groves passed through the back door of time," Matt went on. "All that stuff you hear — phantom towers, pirate radio beacons — that's science-fiction."

Valerie picked up her guitar. "Then what's true?"

"That Mr. Groves was a war vet and he was lost," he said. "That he flew away to find peace."

"That's one possibility."

"He could be alive. Maybe he ran away for reasons of his own."

"But why?"

"To look for God," said Matt, but he didn't sound convinced.

Valerie's hands plucked the strings, finding their way into a melody. "Sometimes I dream about his plane," she said. "The day it took off."

"You should write a song, then," he replied. "It deserves a song."

She started to *la-la-la* a tune, but all she could hear were the clocks.

* * *

Valerie remembered a few lines of the song she wrote:

Take me to far lands, take me to silent lands, bright wings of silver, stars in the night's design.

Dreaming of visions, rainbows and prisms, freedom from my prison, lost in my island time.

* * *

Mr. Reilly's clocks were ticking, rattling her bones. "You want to see them?" Matt asked.

His house on Groves Island was so dark indoors that smells were amplified, the way that creaking sounds at night seem louder and more threatening than they are. To a teenage kid, the place smelled dangerous, reeking of killer chicken grease from last winter's soups and Vicks Vapo-Rub from January's chest colds. Mrs. Reilly was sickly, a victim of polio who walked with a limp *and can't clean every day*, said Valerie's mom when she complained of the odours. *Try to understand.*

She'd just try not to breathe.

In the shadowy living room, the furniture looked as if it might have roots. It was as soft and lumpy as a colony of mushrooms. An ancient Victorian sofa, two wing chairs, two china lamps with tasselled lampshades and a bookcase jammed with ancient-looking books. No clocks.

"Don't look so hard," said Matt. "Listen."

The bookshelf was ticking — *thunk, thunk* — slow and deliberate, like an elephant's pulse. On it was a large tome with numerals and hands. The time was wrong. It read "Seven."

"It's July," said Matthew.

"Huh?"

"Seventh month. It's a year-clock."

A gleam caught Valerie's eye, a dazzle of light on glass, impossible in a room so dark. She thought that Mr. Reilly must have positioned a lamp to light this beautiful thing, this perfect glass cube on the mantelpiece, its tiny, meshing gears shimmering like cut jewels. On its glass face, two silver, needle-thin hands were spinning backward, then forward, as if uncertain of direction, sometimes swooping in a circle, clockwise, then counter-clockwise. Mad and exquisite and senseless — she was in awe of it until she realized that the numbers on the face were random.

"That doesn't make sense," she said.

"Sure it does. Time can get broken and run all crazy."

"Like when?"

"Like when you're dreaming. Dad's working out the mathematics of dream-time."

Really useful, she thought. *Bulova Dream-Time.*

"Random numbers interest Dad," said Matt.

One of the chair-backs held a clock-face, set to a time zone that didn't exist.

Matt kicked aside a hooked rug to show her a clock built under a moveable panel in the floor. It looked like a safe, only the combination dial was the clock, and each of the three numerical turns adjusted for the various aberrations of sidereal time.

A star-clock under the floor.

"This is nuts," she said.

"My dad says the world's gone crazy," answered Matt.

"This is supposed to make it sane?"

He shrugged.

What unnerved Valerie most was the fact that each clock had a name, engraved in brass. Mickey the Fist, said one. Junior; Whiz Kid; Charlie Chan. Nicknames — she thought of war buddies as she glanced again at the dream-clock made of glass. Its label bore a full, majestic name: *Jeremiah.*

On the mantel was a framed photograph of a group of men in uniform, her father among them. He was nicknamed Jerry, but Jeremiah was his name.

* * *

It was a strange memory, as if crazy Charlie had set the table for a global potluck supper of anarchy and madness, and Valerie imagined time bent out of shape by fake clocks, by swerving gyrocompass needles, by the law of gravity suspended, by planes vanishing into some other sky. *Poor soul,* she thought. Who knows what rage Charlie felt at her father's death, what goodness he might have seen in a man she'd hardly known.

Only young Valerie didn't see it that way. She told her mother, who tried to explain that the odd clock was a unique and loving tribute to her father, a man who died of sorrow from the war, but Valerie said, *it's a make-believe clock* and besides, *he died in an accident, not the war.* Her mother frowned. *There are no accidents in this world*, she said.

* * *

Valerie walked up to Matt, reading on his back stoop, in the consoling stillness of his grove. When he saw her, he put down the book and stood up.

"You okay?" he asked.

She'd come back to tell him that her father's name on the glass clock had upset her, but the words broke on her tongue, and she hid her face in her hands. She didn't want him to see her crying. Tears made her afraid, as if they were an acid bath that would eat away at her skin and bones. Matt took her in his arms. He stroked her hair and rocked her back and forth as she wept. *Oh, baby,* he whispered, *this world is a sad, sad place.*

* * *

The TV commentator's voice drifted into Marguerite's living room. He said that there would have been a fireball. It could have shot down the elevator bank.

Firefighters were broadcasting on a frequency of nerve and bone, the only channel left open to the world. *We have no way of knowing what's up there. If the stairwells are passable. Which was the impact floor. Who is alive below it. If there's any water.*

Valerie remembered Robert's words. *Un accident.*

He sat bent forward, face in his hands.

* * *

There are no accidents, wrote Matt once. *God holds us in his loving care. Only it seems that God "lets" bad things happen. That's our point of view because we live inside of time. God has no "plan," no hour, month or year from now. God just is.* Yet Matt loved time and the hours, the ancient clock of daily prayer, the Church and the world as its two great hands. *Prayer is a form of energy,* he wrote. *The air humming with voices. God listens, so we must listen, too.*

The phone rang and Valerie lifted the receiver.

"Hello?"

No answer.

She thought it odd, that it would ring just then.

17

VALERIE FELT MESMERIZED by that seaman's watch of
Robert's. The act of remembering was trancelike, in its
rhythmic to-and-fro. Needing fresh air, she stepped outside
into Marguerite's garden, into its dazzle of sunlight, its tidy
rows of staked tomatoes, fresh lettuce, green beans trailing
across a latticework of poles and string. Inside Marguerite's
soul she stood – within her gardener's precise and measured
way of looking at the world, its practical mix of rigour and
beauty.

Finding a basket, she crouched down and began to pick a
few tomatoes. The fruit was lustrous, ripe with the pungent
scent of sun and warm earth. *Tomato-ness*, as James would
say. *There simply is no other word for it*, and he'd contemplate
that ripe fruit in his hands like a king admiring a jewelled orb
of the world. The thought comforted her.

She herself made a good living cultivating frivolous plants
— lupines, delphiniums, roses and hollyhocks, cascades of
beauty that came and went. Her mother, who'd loved flowers,
preferred to leave them alone. Chicory and Queen-Anne's-lace
had crowded her garden, choked out by black-eyed-Susans and
the chill of autumn. Her wildflowers found their own order,
their own patterns of colour and form. From their vitality,
Valerie had shaped her idea of a cultivated garden. It was Matt
who'd loved the wildness.

He'd come to visit, sitting beside her on the old wooden bench, his gaze intent, plucking daisies, threading them through her thick plaits, kissing her on the lips. He would never have believed that someone could crash a plane into a building. *I've come to understand that we are better than our own worst acts,* he'd written to her as a priest. *I guess we'll have to revise that script,* she thought. *Look at these beans.* She snapped a small one off the vine and bit into it. It *tasted* green. The best time to harvest and to eat was always right now, in all its sweetness. She snapped off a second bean, enjoying its crunch, its taste.

Matt wasn't hopeful as a young man. Fair and slim with pale blue eyes, passion trapped inside of them like a hiss of flame in a kerosene lantern — he was the neighbourhood kid who loved her, who was troubled because the world was tipping over on its side like a derailed freight car with a toxic leak; because in spite of his father's sacrifice in the war, thugs of every stripe tossed matches into flammable villages in Vietnam; because in New York City in 1970, anarchists in the Village made a fatal blunder and dynamited their own house, endangering everyone on the block and killing themselves in the bargain; because a few weeks before that, terrorists in Switzerland (of all places) had bombed the luggage bay of a passenger plane, blowing it out of the sky.

* * *

Yesterday — before the attacks and the onslaught of memory — Valerie had plopped beans down into the bushel, joined by an acorn squash or two. There were squash-flowers on the vines that needed to be plucked. It was too late for them to set fruit, but the blossoms were luminous, huge and golden, too lovely to discard. She'd decided to bring one inside, to float it in a bowl of water. Cupping her hands around a bloom, she could feel it humming. A bee was drinking nectar from the pistil, carrying pollen on its hairs, stopping to refuel as it moved from flower to flower with its strange, erratic pattern of flight. What stillness, what mastery of the impossible, she thought — the zigzag movement of bees was an aerodynamic mystery, a path that belonged to their fullness of life, to the scents of her mother's garden, to Matt drifting toward her, wrapped in silence.

They were both eighteen when he took her hands in his and asked her, "What do you want in life?"

"Love and music," Valerie replied. "Children."

His face got the look of a ragged sky, a dark cloud in its grip.

"You want to bring children into this world?" he asked.

"I'm not going to raise them on the moon," she said.

Matt didn't answer.

* * *

Years later, Valerie wondered how love had come to them. Yet now it seemed to her that each had managed to get lost in the other's imaginings, that the carved wooden bird and the wild clocks had enticed her with their strangeness, and that likewise, her love of flowers and her singing in the dark woods had become for Matt both a solace and a dwelling-place. Together they were building a home of beautiful conjurings, a place of nurture and so, she believed, a place that was meant for a child. It had troubled her, that Matt would question this.

* * *

Valerie went back inside, eyeing the garden from the kitchen window, the leafy outdoors merging with the intensity of colour on the windowsill. On it sat the golden flower picked from the squash vine, its beautiful trumpet floating in a glass bowl.

It was joined by a blue-edged coleus, a glossy philodendron, the striped cascading of a spider plant. Valerie watered each of them, feeling the glaze of light on each leaf, light sinking into every pore, buttery light into her skin, the warmth of human touch, Gerard's. *You are welcome to my home,* he'd said. His French accent struck her ear like a brisk wave hitting sand. *I hope you will enjoy Toronto.*

Unlike her mother, he kept his garden at the front of the house. Purple gentians and lupines stood against a brick wall in the late-noon sun — flowers that appeared tidy and masculine, even the white hollyhocks that cupped the light and spilled it into the lengthening day. *I have not much time for this,* he said, meaning the garden, and he eyed the flowers with the pensive look of his youth. *I hope you will find them calming.* His eyes looked concerned, their gaze resting on Matt's hand, the weight of it on her shoulder.

A day or two later he asked her, *are you happy to be here?* Her stomach tugged at the question. It clenched its fist of a life. *I'll be even happier if things go my way,* she thought.

Of course, she said aloud.

* * *

That clutch of life inside her was Matt's child, and she wanted children, and she was all of twenty, almost through with college, but the world was in trouble, or so Matt thought, and in a year's time, he'd be in Vietnam. Not for him, dodging the draft, not even for his own child. *Think of what that would do to my father,* he told her. *Telling him he was a sucker, to suffer what he did.* Valerie said *it's your child, too,* but he begged her to understand. He said, *If I don't make it back, it won't have a dad,* and Valerie had wept and said, *Please don't go, we can get married and run away to Canada.* But he kept saying he couldn't let his father down, and if she quit college, she'd let her mother down, and her mom would kill both of them if she found out what had happened.

I love you, sweetie, he whispered. He ran his finger over her lips. It felt like a warning.

They've changed the law in New York State, he said. *You can have the procedure here,* but Valerie had friends in nurses' training, her Aunt Ann was a nurse, and she was worried her mother would find out. Distressed, she confided in her sister Karen, who had a friend in Toronto, a nurse named Rita who could help her. *Matt's right,* she remarked. *It's a new world. You're still in college, your whole life is ahead of you.* Even so, Valerie felt grieved. She realized that motherhood was the life she'd wanted, the life she had ahead of her.

As she thought about the plan, her mood brightened. It seemed that Rita's house was a haven for Americans fleeing the draft, a place where runaways could rent space from a congenial landlord until they and their partners got settled. Valerie hoped that a kind and supportive atmosphere might inch Matt away from the tangle of guilt he carried for his father's suffering. She hoped he'd come to love their unborn child.

How hard it was now, fearing for her son, praying he'd escaped a fiery disaster, his heart beating in hers, as close as breath. *Breathe,* she told herself, her heart racing. Even as she watered the plants, that moment of light had vanished.

18

WORRIES COME BACK *to you all at once*, she thought. It was no good burrowing into the past, as if that might provide some shelter from the fears of the moment. Memory was too aggressive. It would root you out with a wild growl, sniffing and pawing at the ground. It would make you afraid. Worried as she was about Andre, it did no good to remember Matt. She'd only be frightened for him, too.

She called Chantal in Paris to tell her she'd heard from Gerard. While she did this, Marguerite hoisted herself up on a barstool by the stove, finishing the soup she'd started making before these crazy people did what they did, and now she was keeping an eye on the *hiss* and *pop* of oil, stirring artichokes and onions into the frying pan, glancing at the TV.

"I am losing count of planes," she said when Valerie returned.

"Don't tell me, please."

"Another one captured. I think a different one has crashed someplace."

"Gerard called Chantal. She was so relieved."

"*Oui? C'est bon.*" Marguerite poured chicken broth into the soup pot, added the sautéed vegetables and lowered the heat. "Taste it, please." She handed her the spoon. "Does it need more salt?"

"It's fine."

"I am almost out of cream."

"I have to go into town," said Valerie. She offered to buy some.

"*Merci.* Go to the *fromagerie*, and you can also buy me some Camembert and Boursin."

"I have to check my email. Andre might be—"

"*Oui, je comprends.*"

"I have to find him."

"You need to find a computer. Ask in town."

"You asked me to buy—?"

Marguerite sighed. "Buy whatever cheese you like, *ma chère.* It's all good."

* * *

Take your time, said Marguerite. *The cream goes in at the last minute. We will eat lunch whenever you wish.* In her words Valerie could sense the need for a few quiet hours, space away from so much anxiety. Robert offered her his car, along with a picnic cooler to refrigerate the cheese and cream, *so that you may sit by the water, in the sun,* he said. *It is sad to waste a nice summer day.*

And what will I do by the water, she wondered. *Loll around and sunbathe? My son may be trapped in a fire. My son is missing.* She remembered Gerard on the phone. *Move your fucking ass. Now,* he said to Andre, and her husband's bluntness was a relief. For sure she'd find a computer, not a common thing in Saint-Pierre, but someone would let her borrow one, maybe the owner of the *fromagerie.* She hoped her cell phone would pick up a tower. St. Pierre was a thousand kilometres from anywhere, and it was she who'd chosen this remote retreat at the wrong time.

Blaming yourself won't help, she thought.

Across Rue Amiral Muselier she drove, down a steep hill dizzy with bright houses, and into the centre of Saint-Pierre.

Valerie parked, then walked through the old town, its cobbled streets like tipsy sailors, sloping this way and that. She edged her way along narrow sidewalks, shadowed and empty. The shops were quiet for a weekday.

Only nothing looked the way it should. Streets appeared too steep, roofs tilted at rakish angles, like sassy hats; perspective collapsing into buildings too large, too small, too flat, too distant. She wondered if she could walk without tipping over, if she could judge the time it would take to cross the street without getting hit. She imagined New York's calamity spilling into the rest of the world, its fire and ash collapsing into the steep uphill streets of Saint-Pierre, their flimsy wooden buildings turned to rubble and sliding into the sea. It felt as if the island itself were listing, a ship about to sink.

Then she began to hear the sound — dark and hollow, a single intermittent note of music struck against the noise of cars bumping over the ancient streets. The cathedral bells were tolling, a steady heartbeat, a metronome punctuating the minutes, carving stillness into the day. She'd never heard bells toll before. The sound belonged to another century, to a lost aural landscape, like the ring of a blacksmith's hammer, or the *clop-clop-jingle* of horses in the snow. Dark and medieval, the bells were tolling for the victims of the Black Plague, for unseen bodies smouldering on pyres, for all souls, living and dead.

After a while, she couldn't hear the bells, unless she paused to listen.

The town felt subdued. A few American flags fluttered from the cabs of trucks, from the back seats of *motobicyclettes*. At the bottom of the hill was a TV shop, *Le Salon Électronique*, an array of screens in its window, each with its ugly stamp of black smoke and fire, each with the same images of frightened people running. A crowd had gathered to watch. People were murmuring, drying their eyes.

"*Un avion est écrasé*," said the newscaster. Another plane had crashed.

"*C'est une répétition, peut-être,*" a rerun, maybe, murmured someone.

Valerie didn't care to know which it was.

Then she saw Gerard. A troop of Gerards, one on each screen, walking through the crowd, mike in hand, asking questions of people in flight, but the announcer was doing a voice-over and Gerard was mute. *Maybe he's looking for Andre,* she thought. She stared at the multiple of her husband. All the Gerards looked ashen, as slight as pencil marks about to be erased.

* * *

At the edge of the crowd in front of the shop, she noticed a man who looked like an airline pilot. She couldn't have said why she thought this. Someone else might have taken him for a professor. He was slim, sunlight toying with his blond hair, eyes both gentle and intent, their light a harsh flicker of worry and fear as he watched the TVs in the window. It was his focused look, so caught up with movement and speed, that made her sure of his profession. Gerard also liked flying, but his life in the sky seemed as accidental as the fate of pollen adrift on the wind. Not so this man. *What must he be thinking?* she wondered. He turned to look at her.

"A friend of mine flew today," she said. "From Boston."

"Dear God."

It was the tender way he said it, his words falling into the well of her fear. They made her think of Mr. Groves, the lost airman. Perhaps he'd returned to reassure her. Just now, as if time itself had been bent out of shape, struck down.

The man had an airline logo on his shirt pocket. *See, he's a pilot. He would know about these things, that's all.*

She walked away.

Maybe he was an apparition. Matt sending news.

*　*　*

Who knows where Matt is? she thought. She imagined him at Logan Airport, boarding his plane, finding his seat, adjusting his seat belt, hearing the smooth click of the buckle, then reaching up to turn the knob that regulates the air flow. He'd glanced at his watch as the plane taxied down the runway, reaching for whatever book he'd shoved in the pouch in front of him. Something serious, pastoral theology or social justice. Up ahead, the video ran through the safety procedures — a woman's smooth, dream-whip voice backed by a cheery soundtrack. He registered her message: *should you have to evacuate, the floor lights will guide you along to the beat of the bouncy music and we'll all have a fun time riding down the slide.* He went back to his reading. As the plane reached its cruising altitude, he began to hear the wild, frenetic ticking of the clocks, time running through the hourglass, running in the wrong direction or in no direction at all, and these were the same sounds she'd heard at the very same moment, walking uphill on the Rue Maréchal Foch, *tick-tick-tick-tick* as the pilot announced that a light breakfast would be served. Matt was seated in Business Class, and up ahead, the flight attendants were manoeuvring the trolley, preparing to serve coffee and croissants to the First Class passengers. A man got out of his seat, moving in slow motion toward the woman at the trolley with her back to him. Matt figured he was off to the washroom — a tight squeeze around her. Only the man shoved the flight attendant aside and knocked her over. There was blood, and Matt realized that the man had stabbed her. He saw the flash of a knife, and in an instant, his hands remembered the chill grip of a gun, how it had felt in the war as mercy fled him, as the enemy's body thudded to the ground. Horrified, he watched as the assailant yanked the keys from the flight attendant's pocket and opened the cockpit door.

Valerie kept walking. She couldn't continue imagining this. She wondered where that man had gone, the pilot.

19

THE SOUNDS OF TOLLING bells grew louder and darker. To Valerie's ear, they took on a hardness, like the *clank* of a hammer on the metal stakes of a graveyard fence. *Matt, Andre, James,* it rang. She thought of Gerard's image multiplying like a cancer cell. Three planes had attacked her native country. No, four. An infinite number, if she counted the replays. No one knew how many.

My loved ones are asking to be remembered. That's all.

A graveyard fence, a garden fence, you could only conflate the two on a day like this one when the fist of memory punches a hole through time. Even so, Valerie wondered why particular memories were so insistent, all the while knowing that the answer to her question was ineffable, was lodged like a bullet in her flesh, the wound that had brought her to Toronto. There to the house with its old-fashioned garden fence, its wrought-iron gate with a lift-up latch, its hard, smooth touch cooling her hands. The gate had a fresh black coat of paint, she remembered that. *I hear the super's a bit of a handyman,* said Matt, his slim fingers raising the latch out of its slot, swinging open the gate. A narrow, brick row house downtown, a tree-shaded street near the university, and she walked up the front steps with him, admiring the batik in the front window, the white gabled roofline, the wood-frame porch. *Some nice digs,* said Matt. *This place is close to everything worth seeing,* as if they were tourists. She didn't care. A knot of sorrow ached inside her, three months along.

The front door was solid oak, prim as a church, with carved trim and an antique stained-glass pane. Matt knocked. The woman who opened it introduced herself as Rita. "Welcome to Canada," she said.

Their landlord Gerard was working late; she'd show them their room. Valerie eyed her. Short, black hair, bright eyes, a smile that was high-beam brilliant, like the lights of an oncoming car.

* * *

The things you remember when you're terrified, she thought.

She wanted only one thing: to know her son was safe.

The road tipped downward, as if gravity had had enough of holding up the town. *Yesterday it hadn't been so steep.* Too many thoughts were tugging at her. Uncertain of the zigzag streets, she was looking for the *fromagerie,* feeling Matt's arm on hers, his touch saying, *Rita's been waiting for us,* and Valerie placed a hand on her stomach, as if to protect it from quicksand, an open maw in the earth.

That first evening in Toronto, Rita was making supper and she said, *We're a small group right now. My partner's a draft resister, too, a teaching assistant at the university. He's not around much, but he can advise you on whatever you need to know.* Matt looked uncomfortable until she asked him where he was from, and he said New York City, and she frowned, then asked about muggings. Matt said, *Mugging keeps me in shape, just call me Captain America,* and then Rita picked up a knife and began chopping carrots with such force that one or two of them ricocheted off the wall. *Pop-pop.* Like cars backfiring.

Valerie pushed her memories aside, remembering where she was. *The traffic here is unbelievable.* Everyone in Saint-Pierre was trying to run errands before the midday rest, a custom brought from Europe to this chilly rock of an island. Up ahead was the *fromagerie* on Rue Albert Briand. *One-half litre of cream,* Valerie thought. *A kilo of butter. Any cheeses you like,* said Marguerite. *Three hundred and fifty grams is more than enough.*

She glanced at her watch again. It was past noon.

* * *

Thoughts kept breaking in.

"You haven't met Gerard yet," said Rita. "From Montreal."

There was something uneasy in the way she spoke those words, the way she placed them, one at a time, like small weights on the soul.

"He's only here until he sorts himself out."

Matt and Valerie looked at each other. Wasn't he the landlord?

"You'll have to be patient with Gerard," she said.

* * *

Fromagerie Leduc, the sign read. A handwritten note was taped to the door. *Ouvert toute la journée aujourd'hui.* Open all day today.

That's odd, for Saint-Pierre, she thought.

Monsieur Leduc was behind the counter — a dark-haired, round-faced man with a kind but introspective gaze. He was serving a customer, and he glanced up at Valerie. *Have a look,* he said, pointing to the display case. Behind the glass were rows of cheeses — Boursin, St. Paulin, Camembert, Neufchâtel. None of them tempted her appetite.

I hope he'll know where I can check my email.

On the countertop was a plateful of business cards. *Usine de la Paix,* read one. Peace Factory — it sounded like a place Andy Warhol might have opened in the sixties. *Poterie.* Marguerite had been a potter once, *but no clay could survive my two boys,* she said. With the kids grown, she'd switched to collecting pottery and now she sat on the local *conseil des arts.* The owner of this shop would be acquainted with Marguerite, would at least know her taste. *A good place to buy her a gift.* Valerie took a card.

She heard Monsieur Leduc's voice. "A brie wheel, *c'est une bonne idée.*"

His customer wore a trim navy dress and heels, a leather purse slung over her shoulder.

"I'm filling it with *confiture aux abricots,*" she said. "And sliced almonds."

"I will sample it tonight, then."

"You've heard about Laurent Sarazin?"

That must be Lisette, thought Valerie.

"Such a shock," said Monsieur Leduc. "A young man."

Valerie decided not to introduce herself. The *brie aux abricots* sounded wonderful. She just wasn't up for chatter.

James, she thought, *are you listening?*

Can you get the recipe? he asked.

Tonight I'll ask Lisette, she promised him.

* * *

Monsieur Leduc's TV was on. Valerie saw fire.

She felt something ominous humming in her bones — a police transmission, a chopper moving away from the burning tower. *The top of the building's glowing red,* said the pilot.

Like cigarette ash before it's flicked.

* * *

America's young are on the run.

Of all the things to remember, thought Valerie, but Rita's voice was rich in undertones like the plucked string of a guitar,

99

a note that hummed with the resonance of Andre, now on the run with James and thousands of others. *It's that damn war bringing all of you here.* Rita spoke above a whisper, a conspiratorial tone, her eye out for Matt who was freshening up for dinner. She set out a stew, a salad, a loaf of fresh bread. *Now really, I like Americans*, she said — just as Matt walked into the room.

Valerie heard the sound of a key in the door, the click of a latch — Gerard was back, heading upstairs for a shower, a trickle of sound against the flow of Rita's words. She spoke to them about the house, the neighbourhood, where to buy groceries.

"Maybe you could tell me more about your plans," she said.

"I think you know why we're here," said Matt.

"Yes."

"To visit. Not to stay."

Rita looked puzzled. Her eyes widened like a camera's shutter in need of light. "I guess I just assumed you'd planned to—"

"No. We're just here for—"

Rita looked embarrassed. She smiled at Valerie. "You and me'll have a girl-talk," she said. "All the details."

"You have a date for us, I hope," said Matt.

Valerie flushed. His insistence felt all wrong, an intrusion on Rita's hospitality.

"Two weeks from now," said Rita.

It was what Valerie had hoped for. Without telling Matt, she'd written to Rita, explaining the situation and asking for a delay.

"Two *weeks*?"

"Don't worry. It's safe."

"We'll be out of here by then," said Matt.

Rita glanced at her watch. She was working the night shift, she said. As she got up to clear the dishes, in stepped Gerard. He greeted them, grasping Matt's hand.

"I am overhearing," he smiled. "I hope you are not leaving so soon."

"Not yet," said Matt.

"We will hide you from the FBI. Don't worry."

Matt didn't answer.

20

LISETTE HAD LEFT the *fromagerie*. As Monsieur Leduc turned to Valerie, he glanced at the card in her hand. "You must go there," he said, as if he were giving her directions. He pointed to a plate. On it were pale, creamy slices of Neufchâtel and St. Paulin.

"Try some, Madame."

She wasn't hungry, even for a sliver.

Even so.

The St. Paulin was mild and buttery, the Neufchâtel piquant. Valerie ordered both. *Don't forget the cream*, she thought. She wouldn't. She never forgot anything because nothing disappears from the world. Her mind still held fast to those evenings in Toronto, to the grief she'd felt at the thought of losing her child.

Nothing had changed.

She asked Monsieur Leduc if Saint-Pierre had an Internet café.

"No, but they will help you at the pottery shop." He paused. "Tell them you spoke to me." His voice was firm, like a policeman's. He weighed the St. Paulin, then the Neufchâtel.

"Four hundred grams is okay?"

The TV showed a wreckage of wings and fuselage, a smouldering building, a wall crushed. *Le Pentagon,* the news crawler said. Monsieur Leduc wrapped the cheese and took the cream from the refrigerator. Then he watched the TV, his face darkened with sorrow.

"C'est terminé," he whispered.

On the screen, a tower collapsed in a dark accordion of noise, and in seconds, it vanished from the earth, taking with it the precious music of a thousand souls or more. Only this cacophony was the opposite of music. It was the ugly, dissonant crash of a huge hammer smashing up a piano, all notes sounded at random and at once.

Valerie imagined a cordon of yellow tape encircling the world.

Andre had fled one of those towers. *Which?*

"My husband and my son are in Manhattan," she said. *"Je suis new-yorkaise."*

Monsieur Leduc handed her the parcel. He looked stricken.

She opened her wallet, but he held up his hand. "No, Madame, please. I am so sorry."

At the bottom of the TV screen, the crawler reported that a fourth plane had crashed in a Pennsylvania field.

21

VALERIE KNEW THAT there was no explaining kindness. There was no mistaking how it felt — like rain on dry earth. *We know where we come from,* she thought. *We know it first, of all the things we know.*

Monsieur Leduc would have known New York only from films and TV. *So that is why you need email,* he said. *To find your son.* Staying open at the midday break gave him something to do — weighing, measuring, wrapping parcels with old-fashioned paper and string while the world's cloth unravelled with the pull of a single thread. As Valerie looked at him, she remembered Gerard as a youth, and it was his hand she felt when Monsieur Leduc pressed the package into hers; his kindness, too — how on that first night in Toronto, he'd sensed her disquiet, without understanding its reason.

"I am sure that everything is new to you," he'd said. "But not so different from your country. Except that you are safe here."

"Safe there, too," said Matt. "We're going back."

Gerard paused. "You are lucky, then," he said.

"How so?"

"You are not one of those who have to flee your country."

"Not at all," said Matt.

"Then you are safe from Vietnam."

"I'm *going* to Vietnam."

Gerard said nothing for a moment. His eyes were sad. "I

wish you well, my friend," he said. He turned to Valerie. "It's all right, we will take care of you."

His words had the weight of touch, an instinctive gentleness.

Remembering this, Valerie thought of her son's childhood, how Gerard had shown him this same warmth and kindness. Yet had Andre been alive in her youth, he would not have understood his dad's patience with his mom. At the end of that first evening, Valerie had found herself staring, puzzled, at Gerard's T-shirt — the hockey-stick logo, the red letter C on a blue field, a white H in the middle. She asked him what the letters meant.

Mom, geez, where have you been holed up?

Hold on, Andre — you weren't even born then.

You must be alive. I can hear your voice. You must be.

Gerard had smiled at her. "You don't know? It is nothing I will wear on the street in Toronto."

The Canadiens, *Habitants,* Habs — he was a Montreal fan, he liked to play, and she'd pictured him skating after the puck with easy grace. His father had season's tickets at the Forum, two seats at centre-ice. She knew that Matt liked hockey, too, and she imagined him playing with a grown son, enjoying the *whack* of the puck skidding past the goal line, the scrape of the stick on ice, its glide as sweet and crisp as the autumn air.

When Chantal was eight years old, her dad put her on skates, got her a helmet, bundled her up in shoulder- and shin-pads — a scrap of a kid who took to the ice, whacking away at the puck, hissing with energy like a fizzy pop can ready to explode and poor big brother Andre was no match for her. A comfort, those chill Saturday afternoons, Gerard with the kids meeting their friends, lacing up at Christie Pits, and Valerie would go there to cheer them on with extra scarves and mitts and a thermos of hot cocoa. Innocence gone now, drifting away like the morning fog in Saint-Pierre.

22

L'USINE DE LA PAIX was a few blocks away from the *fromagerie*, but Valerie was in no position to understand what this might mean, how long it might take to traverse the distance, with *near* and *far* shifting before her eyes. Time past was sifting into now, so that what she imagined was a peace symbol, a poster wreathed in flowers on the kitchen wall of Gerard's house, unforgettable for its ugliness — chartreuse, fuchsia, and orange — but it was a birthday gift from Rita, so he had to put it on the wall.

She pushed the image aside, kept walking until she found the place, one of a row of tiny, weathered shops — a bakery, a café, a drycleaner's. Each looked one-dimensional at first — flat, plain and homespun, like pictures of shops, rather than the real thing. As she approached them, they seemed more real but also strange — attached to this narrow street but adrift somehow, like laundry on a clothesline. An old-fashioned neighbourhood — no Starbucks or ATMs, no crazed hijackers or urbane cell phone users sloshing through this backwater of time. She wondered if these shops took credit cards, thinking hers might dissolve in her hand if she pulled it out of her wallet. *Who knows what year I've walked into,* she thought. *1970?*

James would have been alive, at least.

This place isn't closed for the break, either. It's that kind of day.

She stared at the shop, at its maroon façade, its bright blue door, its yellow peace symbol.

I wouldn't go back to that year, even if I could.

She felt in no hurry to go in.

Yet something was pulling her, and she reached to open the door.

Valerie stepped into darkness. She could see phosphorescent stars on the black ceiling above her. *I'm breathing in something stronger than salt air,* she thought. On a table was an incense burner, its cat's-tail of lazy smoke meandering upward, and then a long-haired woman emerged from behind a velvet curtain. She gave off a complicated fragrance. *Gardenia,* thought Valerie. *A touch of citrus and jasmine.* It was the scent of frangipani, a long-lived flower. She imagined it blooming thirty years ago, the moment frozen into now.

The woman's look was vexed and sombre, her gaze disquieting. She wore a high-waisted Indian smock, crimson and covered with beaded embroidery. Her French was good (but not a native's), her accent indeterminate; her voice low-pitched, almost hoarse, as if she'd either smoked or wept too much. She said her name was Rue, but the darkness of her voice made her hard to hear over the noises of the street.

"I'm looking for a gift," said Valerie.

"In front of you," said Rue, "is a treasure."

Before her was a small vessel, one that in ancient times might have held perfume or oils for anointing. The pot was round, glazed in deep blue and gold, the tapered neck of the lid rising from a base of irregular clay circles so full of movement that she could almost feel the potter's wheel spinning under her hand. It had strength and presence, as if it had just been made, and a phosphorescence that was also darkness, like a scattering of galaxies at midnight.

"Where did you find it?" Valerie asked.

Rue smiled. "Long, long ago," she said.

As if *long ago* were a place.

"I remember it." *In Gerard's house,* she thought. *The summer we met. Could it be a pot he had that once belonged to Ora? No — too strange, too much of a coincidence. How would it have gotten here?*

"In your memory, then, is where I found it," said Rue.

Valerie wondered what on earth the woman had been smoking. In a back room, the radio was on. She heard the sound of the towers collapsing.

"C'est un mensonge," said Rue. "A lie. Mass hysteria. An optical illusion."

"I hope you're right," said Valerie.

Rue looked perplexed.

But then, thought Valerie, *This shop might be an illusion. This beautiful pot before me. The whole day, in fact.* The idea was too good to be true.

Marguerite had once been a potter. This was a gift she would love, if it were real.

"Fifty euros, please."

Valerie hesitated. "I know the man who owned this."

"Do you like it?"

"Do you want me to pay for an illusion?

Rue smiled. "Touch it. It is real."

Valerie reached out to feel the familiar swirl of the clay, the tips of her fingers alive with the night Gerard spoke to her about Ora.

Time, she thought, had collapsed upon itself. The day had done this, had flung Ora, her beautiful pot and her death into the present. She could think of no other explanation.

Or maybe her memory was fooling her and it had nothing to do with Ora.

"It's so beautiful," she said. "It's almost music."

"It is yours, then," said Rue. "You are its rightful owner." She found a box and began to pack the clay pot.

"You don't want anything for it?"

"It has been in my shop for over twenty years," she said. "And no one wants it. They say it is too *inquiétant*. Disturbing."

She thanked Rue, then asked her where she could check her email.

Rue's face became clouded, grey as an old winter sky. "You are returning to the world."

To find my son, thought Valerie. Remembering Rue's remark about the towers, she didn't speak.

"Across from the *fromagerie*," Rue whispered. "Look for a seated man with a laptop. *Il est assis à la fin du monde.*" Seated at the end of the world.

Today's really gotten to her. She's not all there. Poor soul. Valerie heard the screen door slam as she hurried out into the eye-aching brilliance of the day. *Maybe I'm imagining things,* she thought. She was clutching the box. *But not everything. Not this.*

23

W E LIVED IN CAREFREE TIMES, thought Valerie, clutching
her parcel. *That's what they say about the sixties, but not
for everyone. Not for Gerard.* The past was in flood through
the wide-open sluice of memory, how one evening in Toronto
Gerard sat, eyes lowered in concentration on his dinner, his
hand fiddling with a day-glo daisy coaster, pushing it around
as if he were trying to shove a puck past the goal line. The
radio was tuned to CHUM, playing "Bridge Over Troubled
Water" by Simon and Garfunkel. Valerie told him it was her
favourite song.

"What is?" Gerard got up, went to the fridge, pulled out a
beer. She mentioned the title.

"I am sorry," he said. "I have not been paying attention to
music."

He lowered his eyes as he said it, as if he wanted mercy.

"It's nothing," she replied.

Yet Valerie knew it mattered, that a guy her own age was
clueless about such a great song. He opened the beer, swigged
it down, fidgeted with the tab, a fork, a knife. He didn't seem
to hear her, and then she felt his gaze touching her skin, as
if he'd never set eyes on her before. His gaze filled up with
wonderment, then — horror. There was no other word for it.
Gerard's shaken look passed and he managed a smile. "I hope
you are enjoying my father's house," he said.

She felt chilled.

"It's a nice house," she replied.

Gerard explained that his dad was a Montrealer, buying up Toronto properties for the day when the *indépendentistes* would come to power and kick the Anglos out of Quebec.

"He lets me live here, as long as I find tenants," he explained.

"So you're the super," said Matt.

"Yes, but I work for the Parks Department."

"Outdoors?" asked Valerie. "That's a nice job for a student."

"Yes, outdoors, but I am not a student. I am graduated since two years."

It puzzled her — a Montrealer with money and a degree, moving to Toronto to shovel up dog poop. Then she remembered what Rita said. *He's only here until he sorts himself out.*

Gerard asked if they were students. Valerie told him she was an English major. "I'm studying journalism," Matt said.

"That is my field also," said Gerard. "I was reporting business news on TV in Montreal."

And now you're sweeping up cigarette butts with a flip-top shovel. What did they fire you for? Valerie wondered.

"This spring, I have taken *congé exceptionnelle*—"

"Leave of absence," she said to him. She was doing a minor in French, but she knew zero about the *indépendentistes* or the extremists who called themselves the *Front de Libération Québequoise*. Yet she could feel a rumbling in his words — an intimation of something about to happen, an explosion, people running from a collapsing ceiling, buckling walls, wires dangling in a mass of rubble and shattered glass, the chaotic floor of an office filled with smoke.

"In the Montreal Stock Exchange, a bomb went off," Gerard began. He spoke in a quiet, measured voice, as if he were giving testimony in court, as if a tape recorder were running. "I was there when it happened. My brother was thrown by the force of the bomb on the trading floor. He hurt his back."

"I read about it in the *Times*," said Matt.

It had happened in 1969, over a year earlier — an attack that drew ambulances, firemen, police; the ticker-tape machine jammed and spewing out the soybean futures report; a bomb that hit a bank of telephones under the visitors' gallery — the traders' lines to Wall Street. It was fortunate that the New York Stock Exchange was closed that day. No Montreal traders had been working the phones.

"Thank God," said Gerard, "for Abraham Lincoln's birthday. Otherwise my brother would be dead."

I guess I know why you moved here, Valerie thought. A business reporter in Montreal would have to cover the Stock Exchange. The sight of it must have overwhelmed him.

Yet he'd waited a year before he left work.

As she thought this, all kinds of switchboard circuitry started flashing in the nosybody centre of her brain, telling her to buzz off, beat it, MYOB, take a hike because of the look Gerard turned on her. It wasn't anguish she saw on his face that evening. It was fright.

* * *

"You've got Frenchie's batteries charged, is all," said Matt. "Enough voltage there to burn the house down."

"C'mon, Matt, you're in J-school. Where the hell's your Snoopy gene?"

"Huh?"

"Aren't you curious about this place? What the hell's going on?"

"You mean with Gerard?" Matt calmed down like a boiling kettle that had just been removed from the heat.

"Why did he wait a year to take a leave of absence?"

Matt shrugged. "Maybe it took a year to hit him."

"A bomb in the Stock Exchange? It would have caught up with him faster than that."

"Nuh-uh. Remember what our dads went through. It was years before it got to them."

"This is different," said Valerie. She just couldn't say how.

24

THE MEMORY SEEPED INTO HER, humming under the surface of her thoughts, hurrying her along.

Having parked a few blocks further south, she found her way to Robert's car, then packed the foodstuffs in the cooler and shoved the gift in the trunk. This felt like an accomplishment. She was afraid that the town's landmarks might have somehow rearranged themselves, spun into bizarre new patterns like fragments in a kaleidoscope. Thinking that she'd gotten used to the skewed perspective, she looped back to Rue Albert Briand, passing again through the centre of town.

As she approached Place du Général de Gaulle, she heard a staccato retort — a driven, insistent, *click-clack, clickety-clack,* trim and brisk as a soldier's march. High heels trotting across the square, a woman's dark hair tossed by a breeze — it was Lisette, her face half-hidden by a huge bouquet of calla lilies, anthuriums, gladiolas. They were spectacular, these enormous cut flowers, bright gold and crimson, tangerine and purple, but to Valerie they also seemed grotesque, each of them too garish and fleshy, each one a caricature of a fragile living thing.

The flowers must be for the party, she thought.

Marguerite's sister looked like a model displaying an armload of blooms.

But how will she fit them into her apartment?

Valerie thought to stop her. She could offer to take some flowers home.

Lisette had turned to smile at an admiring man, as if he were about to take her picture.

Then she disappeared.

* * *

A café across the street from the *fromagerie* — that's what Valerie found out at the pottery shop, but she didn't recall a café at that location. Rue Albert Briand was two blocks away, and opposite the *Fromagerie Leduc* was a dress shop, a travel agency, and a bright yellow clapboard house that looked like a real estate office. Its tiny green lawn and garden distinguished it from the other businesses, yet even so, Valerie didn't recall seeing this building earlier. She noticed a green planter full of geraniums under a lace-curtained window. The curtains were drawn. Next to the front door was a painted tile, the kind that shows either a house number or the name of a business. The white tile was edged in flowers, and in the centre was a bright blue exclamation point.

Too cute, she thought.

Valerie crossed the street, then walked a few metres in the opposite direction, thinking she might have missed the café. When she turned back again, she noticed a man and a woman coming out of the yellow house. They were each carrying moulded-plastic tables that they set up on the sidewalk. They went back for the stacking chairs, working until they'd set up four tables. On their last trip inside, the woman returned with two cups of coffee and the man came back with a laptop. Then he sat down.

"Welcome," the woman said to Valerie. "We are Jeanne and Michel Brunet."

"I didn't know there was a café on this street."

"There isn't." She pointed to the tile by the door. "We open on impulse."

Like a lemonade stand, thought Valerie. Years ago, she and Karen used to sell lemonade and old comic books from a wooden crate that their mother set up in front of the house on Willow Road. Only this was different. You couldn't just run a café when you felt like it. You needed a license and a visit from the Health Inspector. You were supposed to post a menu. The world hadn't changed *that* much since this morning that these rules would be suspended.

Valerie remembered why she'd come.

"Have a seat," said Jeanne.

"Would it be possible for me to check my email?"

Michel got up and pointed to his place. "*Mon plaisir.* I must attend to my other clients."

There was no one in sight.

The man went inside. Jeanne followed him. She returned with four small vases full of chrysanthemums, one for each table.

"Would you like something to eat?" she asked.

Valerie ordered *eau gazeuse.*

"You are not hungry?"

"My son is missing in New York."

"*Je suis desolée.*"

Jeanne brought her some sparkling water, then went inside. About to log on, Valerie glanced at the laptop, at the white, sunlit table crossed by a long shadow. Standing before her was the pilot. He looked at her with troubled eyes.

"You are busy," he said.

"I must find my son." Her hands rattled the keyboard. "Please sit with me."

She was afraid to receive bad news alone.

A slow connection. She had a moment to find out who he was. His name was Jean-Claude and he worked for Air France.

He'd flown from Paris to Montreal, then booked a local flight for an excursion to Saint-Pierre before returning home. Now he was stranded, unable to fly. When Valerie told him that she was from New York, he pulled out an address book and pointed to a name.

"My sister-in-law," he said. "I have tried calling, but I cannot reach her."

"She's in Brooklyn. She's safe."

"My brother is not safe." His brother worked in one of the towers, he explained.

"He might have escaped."

"*Mais oui.* We are so close, my brother and I. We often walk in Central Park, along the *grande allée.* He might have gone there."

"He may be trying to email you." She glanced at the screen.

"I am interrupting."

"No. A remote connection. Much too slow."

"Only last week, I saw my brother in France," he said.

Anxious now, she asked him about his family. His children were grown, he said. She watched his eyes as they moved across her hand, as they paused at the ring on her finger.

"Where is your husband?" he asked.

"He's in New York, also."

"He is all right?"

"He's gone looking for our son," she said.

"Your son is missing?"

"I'm sure they'll find him." Her voice seemed unnatural to her, too bright. "I'm sure there'll be email."

"Forgive me. I mustn't stop you—" Jean-Claude looked away, the pain in his face undisguised. "It is insanity," he whispered.

"We'll be all right," she answered, unsure what she meant, or what anything meant — two fearful strangers, a sidewalk café on a deserted street, the silence wracked by a tolling bell.

"If I were home, I'd be working in the garden. Keeping busy."

"Yes, there are things we must do at times like this," said Jean-Claude.

"What must you do?" she asked.

"I must fly," His voice became intense, as if he meant right now. "It will make all the difference in the world."

"Will you find—?"

"I want to answer these people back."

She imagined fighter-planes, and the thought distressed her.

"No, I do not want revenge," he said.

Her hands remembered the soft leaves of Marguerite's geraniums, and again she heard her mother's voice, her murmured benediction. *Blessed plant.* Yet the towers burned. She imagined him cleansing the sky of its suffering. Yet after her visit to the Peace Factory, she'd had enough strangeness for the day. She glanced at the screen.

"I'm online at last," she said.

"When you are done, would you share lunch with me?"

She told him that she couldn't imagine relaxing over lunch when her son was missing.

"Of course," he said. "I understand."

"But stay while I check my email." Valerie looked around. The street was empty. The air felt as soft as the inside of a flower. The bells were tolling in the silence.

* * *

As soon as she went online, it felt as if Jean-Claude had dissolved into air.

There were two emails from her son.

The first had an attachment. *Some photos from dad,* read the subject line. It was sent at eight-thirty a.m. Eastern Daylight Time, just before the first attack. *Dad took these yesterday.* The photos included a beautiful view of the North Tower with the Hudson River in the background, the scene Gerard had described on the phone the previous night.

The second e-mail was sent at eight fifty-five a.m. local time, ten minutes after the first plane struck.

I'm safe, Andre wrote. *James is waiting to be rescued. We've spoken. He's bearing up.*

I'm watching this unfold from the adjacent tower. I love you. Andre.

"The adjacent tower" was the one that had just collapsed.

He was out of there like a shot, I'll bet, thought Valerie.

Pray.

Keys tapping under Valerie's fingers.

Cher *Gerard, Andre emailed me just before you spoke to him this morning, before the second plane hit his bldg. Plse keep in touch. If you can't get through on the phone, email me, I can connect.*

She logged off.

Before Jean-Claude could ask what was wrong, she got up and started running east along Rue Albert Briand. Up ahead, she saw a slight figure, her motions brisk. *Click-clack*, staccato of heels on the pavement, a woman carrying a huge bouquet.

Only Lisette was walking in the wrong direction. Not toward home.

25

VALERIE WASN'T SURE WHERE she was going. Then she knew. *I am going toward my son.*

She felt in her pocket, checking her cell phone to make sure it was on. Then she held it to her ear like a child clutching an enormous seashell, toddling along the beach. The ocean filled her head, the roar of an electronic sea as it crashed on the shore of her native city, and she imagined herself a human antenna, pulling in voices from far away.

Officer, I'm looking for my dad.

My buddy, he's a rescue worker — gone, like that.

My brother's a firefighter, pray for him.

To this fragile net of voices, she added her own. *Please help me find my son,* she said into the phone, as if someone were bound to hear. *He's tall and fair and he carries a laptop. He's wearing a grey sports jacket and tie.*

Let us help each other find whomever we have lost.

Through the centre of town Valerie walked, the phone to her ear, striding past the new lopsidedness of everything, the odd angle of the hardware store, the *pâtisserie,* the Place du Général de Gaulle tidy with chrysanthemums; past its small, elegant fountain, its empty benches, none of it looking quite as it should, as if she were comparing this scene to a photo in a travel book, as if memory had deceived her. Clouds had returned to the island sky. Floating above the greyness, its steeple hidden, was a slender metal cross, frail and wire-thin. Valerie started walking in what she hoped was the right direction, toward the cathedral in the Place de l'Église.

The church was close by, and for a cathedral, it wasn't grand; an austere stone-and-concrete building, the colours of its stained glass windows invisible from outside, its clock too slight for the tower's rocky mass. Valerie turned off her phone. It would be impossible to hear it if it rang. All sound had been driven out by the dead weight of the tolling bell, swinging from its ropes like a hanged man. Yet the dark sound didn't seem to emanate from this stone tower. Gazing upward, she walked around the periphery of the church, and although the tolling grew very loud, she couldn't locate its source. It seemed to be coming from everywhere, darkening the town, seeping into the pores of the soil as if the earth itself were tolling.

She felt certain that Andre was here.

As she completed her circle of the church, Valerie noticed a park across the square where a small crowd stood facing the cathedral entrance. They appeared to be swaying in the breeze, gentle as wildflowers lit from inside; a garden full of poppies, cosmos, bluebells, alive with the solemn beauty that plants claim as they grow and die. It felt to her as if these people belonged to this ground, to this particular patch of earth, their roots entangling them, pulling them deep into the soil. The ragged edges of wild asters were alive in the frayed cuff on a fisherman's shirt; the colour of dark maple in the jersey worn by a young man.

Andre, are you here?

A woman wearing a lace collar dabbed at her eyes. She whispered something. "What a shock for the family," and everyone grew silent until the young man in the soccer jersey spoke in a soft voice. "You could not have had a better coach," he said.

Laurent Sarazin, Valerie thought.

"Let us pray also," said the fisherman, "for the repose of the lost souls in America."

It was then that Valerie saw the copper light of a man's hair, the collar of his raincoat turned up; a fair man beside him in a grey sports jacket and tie, a laptop slung over his shoulder. James and Andre stood before her in a human forest without paths, its energy bound into a state of prayer. She slipped into the group, drawing as close as she could to the two men as they clasped hands with others in the circle. She reached out toward her son.

The two men vanished into air.

Where did they go?

They were lost in eternity, in reverent awe, as they had always been.

Alive, she thought.

One afternoon James had brought his art books over for Andre to share, and the two of them spent hours sitting in wonderment, contemplating the sombre icons of Jesus and the saints. *Please come back,* she thought. *Please be alive for me in flesh and blood. Don't sit talking about the richness of the Church or the visible signs of a hidden God, one of them friendship, the other, love. Don't stay there in that memory, that living room of ours. Just come back.*

Only she remembered what Andre had said to James. "How do you — *get* all that," meaning the manifestation of love in the world, and James answered, "I don't 'get' anything. I watch it unfold." As he said this, James gazed at an icon of Saints Peter and Paul, as if he saw some nuance of tenderness between the two men, and he said to Andre, "Did you know they died together as martyrs in Rome?"

"Oh, cheer me up," said Andre.

James laughed.

* * *

She felt a hand in hers. "Don't cry," Jean-Claude whispered. "Come."

It didn't surprise her that he'd shown up here. She was beyond surprise.

The group began to file into church, but she held back.

"This is not for you?" he asked.

She shook her head.

"I understand. You don't have to explain."

She sat on a park bench beside him, closed her eyes, and tried to forget about Andre and James. She could almost picture Matthew celebrating mass inside. If she'd walked into the cool darkness of the nave, she could have imagined him vested, reciting the ancient prayers. Only Valerie knew that since she never went to church, she wouldn't have seen him. Even if he were there.

"My friend who was flying from Boston is a priest," she said. "Have you heard from him?"

"We were lovers, long before."

She wasn't sure why she'd said this.

* * *

They were silent.

"My son and his partner have disappeared," she said at last.

"Don't give up hope, Valerie—"

"Then I saw them in front of the church. In that group."

"They are trying to talk to you," he said.

She drew in his words like breath.

* * *

James once asked Andre if he'd been baptized, and Andre told him no.

"Why not?" James asked.

Because his parents don't take solace in religious bric-à-brac, that's why not, Valerie'd thought, but James said to Andre, "I could baptize you, if you were dying." Andre was intrigued by the thought of ritual anointing and cleansing, and he was struck by the fact that anyone could administer the sacrament to a friend in need. He'd grown up agnostic, but later he decided he believed in God. He loved James for his kindness, but he didn't expect to die soon.

* * *

Valerie felt Jean-Claude's hand on hers. "They have all gone into church," he said.

"Praying won't help," she remarked.

"Flying will."

"You are strange."

"No, listen. At the heart of flying is a still point, a great silence. It is for people who do not—" He folded his hands in a pious gesture, gazing upward.

"Why did you follow me today?" she asked.

"I think you followed me."

"We were both followed," she replied.

He moved to embrace her, but she pulled away. "If you touch me, I'll fall apart," she said.

"I am sorry. I am not thinking today."

"It's all right."

He paused. "What did you mean, 'we were both followed?'"

"We were. By two men who love each other," she said.

He looked at her, puzzled.

"One of them is my son."

* * *

Jean-Claude walked with Valerie across the cathedral square. Then he paused, and gazing far away, he remarked on the clarity of the view, reading the names of one or two shops on Rue Jacques Cartier below them. Valerie, who wore glasses for distance, found his vision remarkable.

"Can you really see that far?" she asked him.

"I *must* see that far," he said, "in order to fly."

Just then, Valerie was distracted by the sight of Lisette. *What's she doing here?* She was going into the cathedral, carrying her enormous bouquet of flowers. Valerie hoped that Marguerite's sister hadn't noticed Jean-Claude, that the huge blooms would block her view. Gossip could start over nothing. She remembered that inside the church, they were praying for the soul of the late Laurent Sarazin. Lisette must have been fond of him, that she'd come here. *Slept with him, maybe,* thought Valerie. *Who knows?*

26

VALERIE AND JEAN-CLAUDE CROSSED Place de l'Église, a few pigeons scattering ahead of them, fluttering away. Above them, the sky was streaked by an oily rag of cloud. *May I meet you again?* he asked. *Later today?* She told him yes, then gave him her phone number. *Neither of us should be alone* he said, *in this dreadful situation.* She knew he was right. Stranded on this island, they shared a particular horror, and yet it seemed to her as if this tragedy were no ordinary thing, that they should not expect anyone to know how they felt. He walked her back to the centre of town, then left.

She felt terrified.

She remembered Gerard, his TV image dissolving into whiteness. Perhaps this gradual disappearance was a form of death — a rain of poisonous ash eating away at him. He was used to covering open warfare, dodging bullets, knowing who the enemy was. He wasn't much for stealth. In this morning's chaos, he wouldn't know how to protect himself. She felt certain that he was slipping away, adrift like a boat unmoored. He'd want comfort, just as she did. *Alone tonight, in New York City.* She turned her cell phone on again and called him.

There is no service available at this time.

Then she wondered why she'd called.

She found herself once again staring at a row of TVs, peering into the window of the *salon électronique* at the foot of Rue Maréchal Foch. *We are certain that all aboard those four planes were killed on impact,* said the chorus of news anchors, one to a screen. *Along with an unknown number inside both the towers and the Pentagon.*

Valerie felt lost. Gone was the old world, the peaceful sky. For years she'd dwelled there, inside the love of family and neighbour. Yet if your neighbour happened to be Laurent Sarazin, you were just as powerless as if thousands had died.

Nothing seemed quite right to her.

It had been hard making her way down this narrow street. There wasn't much of a sidewalk in front of the *salon* window, and pedestrians were merging into the crowd of viewers that had begun to swell and fill the road. Some weary people were sitting on car fenders and on the backs of trucks. It was, she felt, easier to handle dread with a crowd outdoors. In a public place, you were surrounded by the reassuring signals that this, too, was another day — another standard package of twenty-four hours, none of which could be exchanged or rejected because two or three had been damaged in transit. Men were lugging crates full of canned goods, loading trucks with the weight of uneasy fear on their shoulders, hauling this same burden of worry into the *pâtisserie* with the flour sacks. Soon they'd all go home, have dinner, and watch it on TV. Soon it would all be over.

She also watched, imagining that the horror of the day had cloned itself, its images repeating on multiple screens, and then once again she caught a glimpse of her husband, a string of Gerards, wan and pale. He was doing interviews in the street, but she could hear nothing. It struck her as odd that he'd managed to find people who spoke French, who were composed enough to answer his questions. *Your hair is turning white, Gerard. Last night I dreamt this.* On each of the screens, head after head was more ashen than before, face after face reduced to a smudge of grey.

He's got the dead all over him, she thought. *He's disappearing. He is at home with this.*

The idea shocked her.

Une répétition, said a newscaster.

Of what?

As she watched the screen in the shop window, the second of the two towers collapsed and fell.

* * *

The invisible bell was still tolling. A woman was crossing herself.

She remembered Andre's email, telling her he'd called James — *It's okay, fella, help is on the way.* Help never came.

Only she'd seen the two of them at the cathedral. Then Jean-Claude.

Andre, Karen, Chantal. Bone of my bone.

And you, Gerard.

It was over — for now.

* * *

At the bottom of Rue Maréchal Foch, the crowd began to dissolve. By the time Valerie turned around, almost everyone had abandoned the TV shop window, walking away from the smouldering ruins of the towers. The citizens of Saint-Pierre slipped down crooked laneways and side streets like rivulets of water after heavy rain, while their silence pressed itself like a thick fog into the shape of the town.

27

VALERIE DROVE BACK TO the *pension*, thinking about Andre, about Jean-Claude, and her longing for consolation. Here she'd come in search of peace only to find herself entangled in a disaster, her son and his partner missing. How fortunate to have met someone in the same situation, a man who gave her hope. *They are trying to talk to you,* he'd said about her son and James.

Gerard, you keep looking for Andre in that cauldron of hell that never stops burning, but I saw our son in front of a church. It has to do with faith in the unseen. How visible has Andre ever been to us? He is alive. I know it.

She parked the car in the driveway of the *pension*. Robert opened the front door. Looking dismayed, he took the cooler from her hands.

"What is wrong?" he asked.

"Monsieur Leduc wouldn't let me pay," she said.

"But you are crying."

* * *

She felt a breeze, a swaying branch, a leaf skimming her bare arm, as if it were Gerard, as if he were helping her up the stairs and into the *pension*. Reaching out, he'd take her hand and pull her through the fire.

Gerard, we must find Andre.

Valerie, I have never stopped looking.
"Your son, is he safe?" asked Marguerite.

* * *

Only when Ora is safe will I be safe. Gerard once told her that.
Ora's dead, Gerard.
Ora's gone to air, he replied. *Her cells are in the atmosphere.*
Every day we are breathing her.
She was like wind, thought Valerie — a voice softening the
air of his father's house in Toronto. Even now she could hear
Ora singing in an eastern language, her plucked instrument
embroidering its way through a minor key. She listened. The
music was still there, drifting out of Gerard's old room, and
she was nosy, like a cat that follows curiosity to a door ajar
and pushes it open with its head. Peering in, she could see the
glimmer of candles in twilight, Gerard's form blocking her view.

"Just wanted to tell you the music's nice."

He hesitated, then let her into a shadowed, candlelit room,
into the kind of solemnity that pushes a knee into bending, a
hand into making the sign of the cross. On a table was a single
rose in a stem vase and a photo of a fair-haired woman whose
look Valerie might have glimpsed in the mirror.

She caught Gerard's glance at the spinning cassette. "This is
her tape," he said. "What you're hearing is an *oud*. An Arabic
instrument." Valerie listened, her hands doing guitar riffs in
the air.

"The *oud* is where the lute comes from," said Gerard, his
speech distant, formal in manner, like a music teacher's. Valerie
wondered if this singer was a recording artist. Yet he'd fallen
silent, the air laden with sorrow, so she imagined that this
was the voice of an ex-girlfriend, that the two had broken up.
Sensing that he wanted privacy, Valerie got up to leave. "Could
you tell me the name of her album?" she asked.

"There is no album."

"Someday, maybe."

"Never."

"I'm sorry," said Valeric, as if she'd knocked over something.

"It is five months today since my friend is gone."

I was right, thought Valerie. *She left him.*

"She died in a plane crash," he said.

⁋ ⁋ ⁋

"Well, is he safe?" asked Marguerite.

"I don't know. Andre sent me an email just before—"

"Let us get ready for lunch, *ma chère.*"

* * *

Gerard, the candlesticks you lit that night had belonged to Ora. They were made of red clay, of a type that is found in the Holy Land. They were round in shape, like ancient oil pots, with pale inscriptions that might have been flowers or letters. Even Ora didn't know what the designs signified. The candles illuminated a slender perfume jar with a tapered neck, glazed deep blue and phosphorescent gold, spinning with life as if it had just flown from the potter's wheel. It was the most beautiful object in the room. By candlelight, it shone with incandescent fire. It drew me in, as if it, too, were Ora's music.

You must have wanted to unburden yourself, Gerard. You didn't have to let me in the room that night — you hesitated, then decided, yes. You wanted to tell me what had happened.

You told me about your beloved Ora Lévis. Her father was French and her mother Israeli. You'd wanted to marry her, but too many things displeased your parents, her Jewishness being only one of them. Her odd beauty disturbed them most of all. Ora had a strange luminescence, even in darkness. She had

131

silver hair as radiant as the moon, translucent skin, sapphire eyes. To your parents she seemed unearthly, already a ghost marked for death. After the tragedy, your mom and dad felt dreadful that they'd said these things. They understood that you needed to get away from them.

* * *

"Taste this soup, please," said Marguerite.

Valerie sipped a spoonful of its cream, breathing in the fine scent of artichokes and hazelnuts. *"C'est délicieux."*

"Comfort food," said Marguerite in English. "I spike it with Armagnac."

"On your birthday," said Valerie, "I should have cooked."

"Beh, you're a guest in my home." Valerie set the table with china plates, crystal glassware, woven placemats that she admired.

"My daughter-in-law gave me those," said Marguerite. "Sit down, everyone."

Robert joined them. Valerie served the soup.

"She bought the placemats on the Cabot Trail, in Nova Scotia."

Robert opened the wine and filled their glasses. "Speaking of trails, you have not yet told us about your morning hike," he said.

"It was beautiful," said Valerie. "The sky turned blue."

"Oui, ma chère," said Marguerite. "But have you heard from Andre?"

"Start before the soup gets cold," said Valerie. She returned the tureen to the kitchen, taking a minute to warm her ice-cold hands on its surface, hoping Marguerite might drop the subject. When Valerie came back, she caught Marguerite's embarrassed look. She was fingering the woven cloth in front of her as if nothing else mattered.

"You know, we often have weavers visit from the Maritimes," she said.

Valerie felt relieved.

"Monsieur Leduc, from the *fromagerie*, he spent his youth in New Brunswick," added Robert.

"Did you meet him, Valerie?"

"He would not let Valerie pay."

"*Ben, oui.*" Marguerite patted her hand. "He is kind."

The table fell silent.

She poured more wine in Valerie's glass, then put some cheese on her plate. "Look at this, *fromage parfait*. He gives fair weight, *n'est-ce pas?* Always a little extra, too."

Valerie squeezed her eyes shut against the hot sting of pain.

Marguerite pressed a handkerchief into her hand. "It will be all right, *ma chère*. Eat."

28

VALERIE CLEARED THE TABLE and told Marguerite she'd tidy up. She turned on the kitchen TV, watching the news ticker crawl across the screen. *Tous les vols sont annulés.* All flights cancelled.

I'll be here a few more days, she thought.

Marguerite made her way into the kitchen. She read the crawler, too, and her eyes gleamed. "Stranded in Saint-Pierre, you can go to the Joinville disco and meet some nice guys. That'll take your mind off Gerard, at least."

Valerie didn't answer.

"You dance, *oui*?"

"I'm not in the mood. But I met a nice man today, and all I did was walk."

"*Mon Dieu*, and on what street did you find him? Tell me!"

"I met a pilot, stranded here. From Paris." She paused. "His brother's missing in New York."

Marguerite grew still. "Please forget what I said about the dancing."

"It's just someone to talk to. That's all."

"*Ben, oui.* You might as well have company, *ma chère.*"

Valerie caught her insinuation like a baseball, a pitch low to the ground. *Gerard will not be alone, I can assure you.*

It's not what you think, she thought. Gerard was on the job. He'd try to do his work, to be calm, as a good reporter should be. His missing son would be his sole obsession. He would not be fooling around.

The phone rang.

"For you," said Marguerite. She left the room.

* * *

Would you like to join me at the café? Jean-Claude asked. *That odd little one on Rue Albert Briand, where you checked your email.* He could meet her at five. No, better — he'd come by earlier and they could go together. Had she any word of her son? *Not yet,* Valerie told him. *It is the same for me with my brother,* he said. *My sister-in-law tells me there's so much confusion, he might have been swept away in a crowd, safe up in the north end of the city. It's too soon to know.*

Let's hope then, said Valerie.

In flying, I will find hope, he replied.

Soon, she said.

Maybe tonight, if I am lucky. But I am so grateful for your company today, he said, and she answered, *I feel the same, you're helping me get through this.* As she hung up, Valerie entered her own words as if they were a foreign country and she were a refugee. Her son dead. James dead. Her flying away with Jean-Claude, navigating by pirate radio beacons, guided by hidden towers into another dimension of time — disappearing, as Mr. Groves had done, inside a place where memory did not exist. Emptied of the past, she'd start again. That's what Jean-Claude offered her. Erasure, forgetting.

Oh, but it wouldn't happen, couldn't.

Andre and James were in front of the church. They didn't die.

Forget you ever thought that.

* * *

Marguerite stood in the doorway. "Going out?" she asked

"Later."

"Could you pick me some lavender and bergamot?"

"You're making *tisane?*"

"I am making you a sachet for your pillow. So you will sleep well tonight."

Valerie doubted she'd have trouble sleeping. She thanked her.

"It is old-fashioned, but you will see it works."

Valerie could have told Marguerite that her bed linens were already sweet from drying on the clothesline in the fresh breeze. It was only yesterday that she'd yanked the creaking rope toward her, grabbing each billowing sheet, pulling it off the line, piling it into the basket. Later she'd folded the linens, smoothing them into rectangles, each sheet fragrant with the day's good air. Some pillowcases were trimmed with Marguerite's embroidery; others with crocheted flowers. Valerie's bed had the prettiest set, with a pale blue ribbon threaded through a border of lace. She imagined a sachet, redolent of summer. Tonight she'd close her eyes and sleep, resting her cheek against a lost world.

* * *

The attacks will change everything, said the TV news.

Back to work. Platters went on the right side of the dishwasher, small plates in front, salad bowls on the left, glasses and serving bowls above, cutlery in the basket. Whatever else happened, everyday things remained the same. In Marguerite's *pension,* there was nothing vertiginous, no collapse of visual perspective. There was gardening and laundry and a right and a wrong way to load a dishwasher. *Separate the knives from the forks and the spoons,* she used to tell Andre. *Oh, Mom, get real,* he'd say. *Knives go blade down for safety,* she continued. *You think I'll fall into the cutlery and stab myself in the gut?* he said. *I think one of us will cut ourselves, pulling the knives out,* she answered. *Okay, okay,* he replied. *Andre, do you know what happens if you put the spoons in back to back?* Andre broke up laughing. *No, what? Do they have better sex that way?*

They get clean that way, she said. Valerie gave him points for imagination.

Andre picked up a pair of spoons. *Okey-dokey, here goes.* He held them back to back and started playing them, doing a little shuffle with his feet. Fifteen years old, what a kid. Jacket off, sleeves rolled up, running down the stairwell thick with smoke. *Hurry, Andre, hurry.* Her eyes teared up and stung, her hands were shaking, knives, forks, spoons clattering to the floor. She crouched down to pick them up. *Chill, Mom,* she heard him say.

* * *

As she worked, Valerie wondered what kind of a man Jean-Claude was. Lean and fit, as pilots were — a man with excellent vision. His eyes were pale blue, and she felt as if she were looking through him, right into the sky. He didn't wear glasses and he could read the names of shops thirty metres away. Likewise, he'd seen into the depths of her, but his own suffering was open to her gaze in a way that Gerard's was not. She remembered that night in Toronto when Gerard went trawling for the memory of his injured brother because he couldn't bear to talk about his lost beloved.

There were things she understood now, that she hadn't in her youth. One of these was Gerard's way of being vulnerable, yet skittish, of hiding from her eyes. She'd lived so long with shadows, having to guess at the feelings of a man, at what grieved him.

With Gerard, she'd dig things up on her own. She could still recall the date when he told her how Ora had died. July 21st, 1970. *It is five months today since my friend is gone.* That was all he'd said.

Valerie dried her hands, turned around and glanced up at a tea towel that Marguerite had hung on the wall. On it was printed a calendar, its borders adorned with trumpet-vines and blue morning glories. *What month is this?* It seemed strange, that she'd have to remind herself. *September.* A drowsy fog assailed her, as it did once when she was coming awake from anaesthesia, resting in the recovery room of a hospital, someone checking her vital signs. *What day is it?* a nurse had asked her. *Tues*-day, said Valerie, stressing the first syllable as if clarity counted, as if her knowledge of the day of the week could get her out of the hospital faster. *Today was that kind of day,* thought Valerie. *A* Tues*day.*

September was, for the most part, a summer month. *June July August September. Summer in the northern latitudes.* It helped to have context. Calendars and clocks were good things, she thought, especially on such a chaotic day as this one.

* * *

You told me, Gerard, that Ora died in a plane crash. Five months to the day *and so the next day I'd counted back, walking to the Central Library, the old one at St. George and College, tucked into the edge of the university campus. In the microfilm room, I unspooled* The New York Times *on a reel threaded between two glass plates, the page turned right-side-up, my hand cranking past the blur of world national local news: Lord and Taylors Macys Saks Broadway* TV *listings Book Reviews. Front Page, February 22nd, 1970.*

A Swissair passenger plane exploded and crashed yesterday, fifteen minutes after take-off on a flight from Zurich to Tel Aviv, Israel. Forty-seven people perished. A Palestinian splinter group has claimed responsibility.

* * *

Under the sink, Valerie found dishwasher soap. She poured it into the well, closed the machine and turned it on. The cleansing noise was soft and familiar, the dishwasher's water heating up with a comforting *shhhh*. She could hear the TV. Thousands of people had been murdered before her eyes. *Poor Ora*. Her blood a river, from that day to this.

29

*T*HOSE CALMING HERBS. Valerie thought she might need them after all. She should clip them now, as Marguerite had asked. A sleep sachet — what a quaint idea. She felt wide awake, as if sleep had vanished from the world.

Marguerite was sitting in the TV room, her leg on a stool, her eye on the screen, on the hundreds of office workers fleeing up Broadway. Now and then, the camera would zoom in on a single look of fear or grief, a tailored suit or silk tie thick with ash.

"Remind me what herbs you'd like," said Valerie.

"Some bergamot and lavender. A few sprigs—"

"Andre!"

"Where?" Marguerite stared at the screen.

"I saw him."

"Sit down, *ma chère*."

Who else could it be — his unmistakable gait, his skin caked in white dust like a fresh clay casting of a death mask.

Come on, Mom. You thought I wouldn't make it?

"Call him," said Marguerite. "Maybe he will answer his cell phone on TV."

Valerie reached for her phone, then put it aside, distracted by another pale figure striding along, a cameraman beside him. *Is that Gerard?* she wondered. Just as the camera zoomed in on him, the man became featureless, a white silhouette in the darkness.

* * *

Chère *Valerie, listen.*
What is it, Gerard?
In New York, I saw Ora falling from the sky.

* * *

Her hands were chilled, as if she were still turning the microfilm crank, still walking through the quiet back streets of Toronto's Annex to Gerard's house, so prim and sad and well-tended, taking Matt into their room, closing the door.

"Do you know what happened to poor Ora?"

Matt didn't.

"Can you keep a secret?"

* * *

Four planes gone, the newscaster said.

Valerie watched the blue sky close around them, Gerard's candle flickering before that haunted face.

* * *

The commentator said *we cannot defend ourselves against suicide attacks. Unprecedented,* is the word he used.

Couldn't see it coming.

* * *

In the garden, poppies were swaying, lit from within, like lanterns. Marguerite handed her a basket and clippers. "Good medicine, *ma chère,*" she said. *So you won't hallucinate anymore,* her look said.

Valerie picked some lavender and bergamot, their fragrances released by the touch of her fingers, their soft leaves brushing against her. She felt moved by their generosity of scent and warmth, their offerings of comfort. *Gerard's garden was just*

141

as beautiful, she thought. *In front of his house in Toronto. The hollyhocks were blinding white the day I told Matt about Ora.*

* * *

"Gerard's girlfriend was on that fucking plane?" Matt asked.

"He told me 'her plane crashed,'" Valerie replied. "'Five months to the day.' I looked it up."

Outside, a daylily was drinking sunlight. She hoped its beauty would console Gerard.

"Holy shit, it was on the news, Val. How could you not know?" asked Matt.

"I forgot all about it," she replied.

Matt's eyes widened, dismay edging its way across his face. "Jesus, don't you remember? Right around the same time that house blew up in the Village. Anarchists making bombs. Weathermen. They probably supplied those assholes who blew up the plane."

"Poor Ora," she whispered.

"'String 'em all up,' my dad says."

* * *

That summer in Toronto, Gerard told Valerie that he wasn't much of a gardener. "It is just good exercise," he said.

"It's a nice garden," she replied.

"It is all right. You could do as well, I am sure."

How unhappy Gerard was then, thought Valerie. Apart from work or a beer, he never went out. Gardening and maintenance were all he did. Later he'd bring a garden into their marriage as if it were a grave for her to tend.

* * *

Valerie felt a hand on her arm, Marguerite's.

"Do you think that was him?"

"Sorry?"

"Andre. You thought you saw your son on TV."

"I'm certain it was him."

"A relief," she said. "At least we know where he is."

"Gerard is disappearing."

Marguerite looked worried. She patted the bench. Valerie came over and sat down.

"*Ma chère*, what makes you think Gerard is disappearing?"

"I keep seeing him on TV. Each time he grows paler."

"It's the ash, *n'est-ce pas?*

"It's because we were looking back in time."

"*Pauvre* Valerie, you need some sleep."

You stepped through the rip that the planes made in the sky. You were standing by the shore of Lac Lucerne.

"He's just lost Ora," said Valerie.

Marguerite took her hand and held it between hers, but Valerie felt none of its warmth. She might as well have been a speck of pollen-dust, drifting with the breeze to land on the hairs of a bee, or on the moist stigma of a flower, or in the foul ash of Lower Manhattan.

It didn't seem to matter where she ended up.

* * *

Only now she was remembering Matt's face, how it looked when she told him about Ora — like a stone wall crumbling, as if a bomb had scored a direct hit.

"Poor Gerard," she'd said. "He's so unhappy."

"Whole damn world's unhappy, sweetheart," he said.

"Ora was so talented. So young."

"The young get to fight back," said Matt.

"But what can you do when they put a bomb in—"

"Go after them, like our dads did." He paused. "Only this is much worse. These guys'll murder anyone, not just soldiers."

She told him that Ora's death had nothing to do with his going to war, that fighting wouldn't help.

"It'll help," he said. "These radicals are all in cahoots."

"So?"

"If it stops some jerk from blowing up a plane, it'll help."

30

THAT NIGHT VALERIE LAY down beside Matthew, and just before she drifted off to sleep, her body touched a lost soul unmoored from time. She was neither asleep nor awake when the night grew dark and the dim stars made her afraid. She thought it was a dream, what happened next.

Or maybe not.

* * *

She drifts into the sound of the unfamiliar, a voice, an unknown name. *Ora Himel-Lévis*, says the voice. *Spring break, and I am in Zurich*, and her wordless thoughts float through Valerie's sleep; she is off to see her mother who lives in Israel, in Yafo, an old Arab city, a part of Tel-Aviv; she has just come from visiting her father in Paris; she lives in Montreal. *I miss Gerard* — Valerie hears these words as they float above the surface of her dream.

But I have to speak to you, says Ora. *Please listen*. Then Valerie feels awake within the dream, Ora's words as clear as if she herself had spoken them. *I am studying anthropology and English. Someday, I would like to write about poetry and folksongs in the Hebrew language. I am carrying with me a book of Bialik's poetry, very popular in Israel, some of it set to music, so that my mother can help me translate, for my final essay*, and then Valerie, awake or asleep, understands that this is not the present, that a ghosted past has entered her body, a time that is not quite past at all.

Gerard is working, and could not come, says Ora.

I am staring out the window of the plane at the tarmac, she continues, looking at the mechanics, the gasoline truck, the control tower. Klöten Airport, that's its name. I don't like Zurich very much, but I was late booking, and I could not get a direct flight from Paris.

It is almost one-fifteen, so we are ready to take off. I look forward to seeing my mother. How sad that my family is scattered and not much of a family anymore. When I marry and have children, I am going to build us a new family. I plan to help my mother emigrate to Canada, so that she can be with my Aunt Rachel in Montreal. My mother loves her country, but she is sick of conflict. Already we have lost two men at war. My cousin Arieh died in '67, and Aunt Rachel's first husband, Uncle Avram, died in 1948. If I had stayed in Israel, I would be a soldier now.

The flight attendant has asked us to fasten our seat belts. I loosen the belt a little before I pull it around my waist and clasp the buckle. I pull it around a secret. I am three months' pregnant. When I return, Gerard and I will get married. The wedding will be at City Hall because his parents' church will not perform it. When his mother and father get to know me, they will feel better. They are good people. They do not know anyone Jewish, that is all.

The wheels roll, very fast. The sensation of speed is something I love, and under my seat, I feel the lift as the plane takes off. I think of the words to the beautiful song, "Shedemati," "My Field," which tells of a field that is sown with tears, but in the morning, the grain is ready for harvest, and the sickle moves, yunaf el al, all the way up to the sky.

Up over the city the plane banks, but the view is rather dull, so I will read — a book in English, for one of my courses. My place is marked with a photo of Gerard, his graduation picture. English is my third language, and it is tricky. My professor says that many English speakers do not know the difference between "lay" and "lie."

There is a thunk, *the wheels of the plane pulling up.*

Also "like" and "as" are difficult. My teacher cannot stand the English idiom, "like, man" which she says has nothing to do with the word "like."

A thunk *and a* bang, *both of them shake the plane, and I put my hand on my tense stomach to comfort my child. There, there, your grandfather is an aircraft engineer. He says to me, don't worry, Ora, they build these things to last, go back to your reading.*

I begin to study the difference between "fewer" and "less," but the book falls out of my hand. I cannot read, my eyes are watering, I am choking, there is smoke in the cabin. The pilot announces over the loudspeaker that he has asked permission to return to the airport. We are only a few minutes away, so we should stay calm.

I look out the window, I can see the control tower in the distance, but we are going the wrong way. The plane is listing, we are near the edge of Lake Lucerne, veering toward the woods, oh dear God, we are flying much too low....

* * *

After seeing Ora, Valerie woke Matthew up.

"She was here."

"Who?"

"Ora. In this room." She started to cry.

"Oh babe." Matt took her in his arms and stroked her hair. "Lots of dreams loose in this world, babe. Don't believe everything you see."

* * *

Valerie felt a thrashing of anger in her stomach. Later she told Gerard what she'd realized.

How did you know that? His voice was a whisper of dread.

Ora wanted to let me know, is all.

* * *

The New York Times reported that the Swissair black box had been recovered. *Good-bye, everyone,* said the pilot. He explained that the cabin was full of smoke, that he couldn't see the controls. His name was Armand Étienne.

A bomb had been placed in an airmail parcel. Triggered by a barometer, it was set to go off at forty-five hundred metres. It exploded in the luggage compartment. The investigators found wreckage strung across the trees in the forest near Würenlingen, in the northern Swiss canton of Aargau. Their findings included fragments of the shattered hold, a smashed propeller, hats and coats and gloves, a charred book of poetry, a torn snapshot of a young man.

31

GERARD WAS WORKING *and could not come.* Ora's words troubled Valerie. *It was true,* said Gerard when she spoke to him about the apparition or the dream or whatever it was she'd experienced. He was supposed to have been on that plane.

Never again did he speak of it.

Matt had been horrified by Ora's death, by the chill wind of it blowing through their lives. In bed at night, he'd hold on to Valerie, as if a hurricane might sweep them both away. Yet Gerard's sorrow had drifted into longing. He'd look at Valerie as if a lost soul were passing through her, as if her hair were dishevelled and Ora was the wind.

* * *

Marguerite went upstairs to rest, while Valerie returned to the kitchen, retrieved the chilled pastry dough and got to work shaping the crust for the *tarte.* She dusted the bread-board with flour.

This is perhaps the most audacious terrorist attack that has ever taken place in the world, said the TV.

The dough was firm, but pliant enough for Marguerite's rolling pin, a French one made of marble. *What a weapon,* Valerie thought. *It could have saved some lives today.* On her next flight, she'd take one in her carry-on.

She had no choice but to watch the news.

Passengers on one of the doomed planes had counter-attacked. They'd tried to plow the food trolley into the cockpit. Valerie glanced at the rolling pin, then at the dough.

Don't even think it, she thought.

Andre would have. *Ready to roll? "Let's roll!" That's what they said! Grab that rolling pin and do it!*

Cool it, kid.

Lighten up, Mom, he'd say.

* * *

Valerie tore off two pieces of waxed paper. With the palm of her hand, she flattened the dough against one of them, then placed the second sheet on top. She felt grateful for the ease of her hands at work, for the simple comforts they could create. She gripped the rolling pin, and began to press down.

* * *

The TV's on, and before me are solemn New Yorkers, American flags, huge banners. Perhaps they'll be seen from outer space. Perhaps some cosmonaut circling the globe will wonder what sort of terrible day we've had on Planet Earth. We Will Never Forget, *say the signs, and it's almost consolation, that their outcry may reach to the stars.*

I'm old enough to remember when flags got burned. I saw it happen once. There was a guy lighting matches in Union Square, and a crush of students were cheering him on.

"You know him?" I asked Matt.

"That friggin' dickhead? No!" he said.

Flames were catching and spreading, gnawing their way through the cloth and blackening each stripe: red, white, red, white, then the field of blue at its furthest end, star after star after star, and I thought, I don't understand the world. Now with my rolling pin in hand, I understand far less than I did then.

* * *

She wondered who it was who'd lit that match, and, if he were still alive, what he would think today. She thought of Matt, how he'd wanted to kill that guy. She could just imagine the two of them, staking out turf like a pair of cowboys, ready for a gunfight on the pyre in lower Manhattan. As if her mind were a hostel for two lonely men, taking the measure of each other.

Cut the bullshit, she told herself. *Andre's still missing.*

Come to think of it, Matt, you're missing, too.

Valerie pushed her full weight downward, rolling out the dough into a thin and tidy circle. *James,* she thought, *watch how I do this.* She draped it over the rolling pin, easing it into the baking dish. *Practice makes perfect.* After she trimmed the pastry at the edges, she put the dish in the fridge to chill.

32

AND WHILE YOU'RE HERE in my head, she said to James, *talk to me about Andre. You've been such a comfort for him. Keep him alive for me.*

James was a kindly soul, balm for a wound. He had the presence of soft rain. Even imagining him would calm her. *I'm glad my son met you,* she thought. She knew that Gerard shared her feeling. Whenever he talked about James and how good he'd been for Andre, he'd remark on the price that loneliness exacts from the young, how fortunate it was that the two had found each other.

Gerard understood desolation, but he never spoke of his own. Nor did he offer platitudes to Andre. Never did he say *in time you'll meet someone* or *loneliness passes.* Maybe he just wasn't sure, and he didn't want to lie to his son about happiness. *Things will work out,* she'd said to Andre, and James was proof she'd been right. To her mind, it was life's great gift that trouble was worn away by time, just as clumps of rocky soil are broken down by wind and rain.

Yet maybe today would prove her wrong.

She thought about the cruelty of that morning's attacks. *Mortal sin,* Matt would have said as a priest — willful sadistic fantasies, thoughts no one had any business thinking, let alone enacting. *God would forgive,* he'd say, *if one of those men had asked forgiveness.* She doubted that this had happened.

She felt certain that life's good soil would never reclaim their stony deeds, never take them back.

Matt, she thought, would agree.

If he's alive.

* * *

She had no way of knowing if Matt were alive. Yet she was exhausted from worry about Andre, and for that reason, she tried not to be anxious about Matt.

Yet there was so much he hadn't yet resolved, so much he hoped to clarify, so many feelings that went deeper than he might have guessed. Matt's soul had great depth, after all those lonely growing-up years in the woods with his father's clocks, with his poor mother's infirmity. He'd understood how Gerard felt, how lost he'd been all those years ago. Yet he'd been suspicious because Gerard had taken her — and not him — into his confidence about Ora's death. "Come on, Matt," said Valerie. "How many times would he want to repeat it?"

She'd been convinced that what Gerard wanted had nothing to do with her. It was the vision she'd harboured that attracted him — Ora's spirit, trapped and beating its wings inside her body.

"It's not that I don't *like* the guy," said Matt. "I mean, he's okay. He's—"

"Matt, I wouldn't hurt you that way," Valerie said.

"Even so, I wish he wouldn't — look at you like that."

"So do I."

"So don't encourage him."

"How the hell am I encouraging him?"

"Frenchie's got the hots so bad, you could fry an egg on his dick."

"You didn't answer my question," said Valerie. Matt looked

so unhappy that she could see his anguish, as if he'd lost her already. She grabbed his arm.

"Matt, I'm here, I'm yours. Grow up!"

He pulled away, dug into his backpack, pulled out a piece of paper. "My draft notice, see? I leave next week."

"You're afraid of losing me, and you're the one who's running off!"

"Reporting for duty is not 'running off.'"

It is when I'm carrying your child, she thought.

* * *

Valerie pulled out her phone and dialled United Airlines. She waited.

I should have done this hours ago, she thought.

"I'm calling to enquire after passenger Matthew—"

"Are you a family member? We can only give information…"

She hung up.

* * *

She remembered a tap on the door, Gerard standing outside.

"Forgive me, I am not eavesdropping. But you've raised your voices."

Valerie apologized.

"No, no. Just that I could not help overhearing. Matt, my friend, I must talk to you. May I come in?"

Matt shrugged.

"I know it is none of my business, but—"

"But what?"

"Why are you risking your life like this?"

"You need to ask?"

"From the first night you are here, I am wondering. You love each other. Why not stay and get married? You will be safe here."

"No one's safe. Thought you knew that."

"I do not."

"The world's full of thugs, pal, in case you haven't noticed."

For a moment, Gerard was silent. "Well, I do not see the sense of it," he said.

"You don't?"

"There will always be wickedness in the world," he said. "But can you just — desert your beloved Valerie? Your child?"

Matt looked stricken. "There is no child," he whispered.

He pushed Gerard aside and strode out of the room.

* * *

Valerie punched in Matt's number on her cell phone.

You have reached the voice-mail of Father Matthew Reilly, Department of Pastoral Theology, Boston College. My office hours....

Imagine if anyone knew what we'd been up to. All those years ago.

She couldn't leave a message. What she had to say was too personal to leave on a priest's voice mail. *Matt, I've forgiven you.* She wanted him to know that. She tried his cell phone.

We are unable to complete your call.

* * *

Valerie glanced at the screen. She kept expecting Matt to turn up on TV.

I wonder how many women miscarried today, she thought. *Or died with their unborn kids.* She felt sure that if he were to ponder this question, Matt the priest would be chastened. *There is no child.* His own words, long ago.

Matt, she thought, *you were always afraid of life. Even as a kid. Remember in grade school, that bully who picked on me?*

You drank. Later it was drugs. In the army, you were handy with a rifle. Or so you said.

No wonder you became a priest — you had to sort things out somehow.

She'd seen a few priests on the tube today — slim, stocky, black-shirted, Roman-collared — all of them in erratic motion, like insects in a wild garden, darting through swarms of fleeing people, congested airports, crowds in front of a church. Just as she'd glimpse the eyes, the mouth, the shape of the jaw, the priest would always turn away, as if he could feel her eyes on him.

* * *

She took the pastry dish out of the fridge, sliced the apples, scooped the cream into the shell, then placed the apple slices down in overlapping circles. *There's going to be a war,* she thought. *Another attack.* On the stove was a simmering pot of melted butter and sugar for the glaze. She poured the glaze over the *tarte*, then put the dish in the oven.

33

WHILE THE *TARTE* WAS BAKING, Valerie emptied the dish-washer, putting the glasses away in the cupboard, the mugs on the shelf below them. Her eyes panned the TV. A cop told a reporter that they had sniffer dogs to look for people trapped in the rubble. *A canine cop might find James alive,* she thought. Only the officer said they couldn't use the dogs today. Not with so many fires burning.

Andre would have run, she thought. *No need to search for him.*

She stacked up clean china. *The soup bowls go one cupboard over.* Valerie caught a glimpse of a reporter, a cop alongside him, making his way into the pit. *The wine glasses belong in the dining room cabinet.* A smudge against the ashen sky, the reporter looked ephemeral and at the same time worrisome, like a dark shadow on an X-ray.

It could be anyone, she thought.

* * *

Only the reporter wasn't just anyone. His image broke through the frail skin of time, was Gerard as he'd looked the night when Matt had run out the door, ignoring his kind confrontation, the truth in what he said. Moments later, Gerard sat down on the edge of the bed, his face in his hands. "I am sorry," he said. "I do not understand this man."

"It's because of his father," said Valerie. "What he suffered in the war. He doesn't want to let him down."

"But he is letting *you* down. Right now."

Valerie said she understood this, that she'd hoped the trip north might change his mind.

"Matt's due to report next week," she said. "He's going home."

"And you?"

"I'm staying."

"You have this — appointment."

Valerie didn't answer. She glanced at her guitar in the corner, as if the solution to her dilemma might be found in some resonant chord, some elegant bass run. She'd always found refuge in music, in the strange, paradoxical silence at the heart of it, a calm beyond either thought or sound.

"May I sing you a song?" she asked.

Gerard looked pensive. "Yes," he said at last.

Picking up her guitar, she played and sang "Island Time," written in memory of Mr. Groves, the song Matt had encouraged her to write.

He listened. "You sing about the mystery of terrible things that happen," he said.

"I'm so sorry about your girlfriend," she replied.

"You have heard of this incident?"

"I read it in the paper."

She couldn't bear to look at him, her body singed with pain and heat, as if his suffering were fire. He reached out, touched her chin, turned her face toward his.

"Valerie, please don't turn away."

Gerard took her in his arms. She didn't want to pull away, but she did. He held her hand and kissed it, and he left it moist where his cheek had rested.

"You have been a good friend," he said.

"I remind you of her, don't I?"

He embraced her, slipping down to his knees, his face resting in her lap, his hand stroking the curve of her stomach.

He was hesitant. "It is okay?"

She told him yes.

Moments later, they heard footsteps thudding on the stairs. Gerard got up. Matt pushed open the door, staggered in.

"What the fuck," he said.

"Matt, have you been drinking?" asked Valerie.

"I've been *thinking*, is more like it," he answered.

"About what?"

He glared at Gerard. "Didn't waste any time, pal, did you?"

"Oh come on, Matt," said Valerie.

"You, of all people," he said to Gerard, "should understand why I'm heading out."

"Well, I don't."

"No? Girl gets killed, fucking plane blown out of the sky, crazy shit's taking over the world, and you don't?"

Gerard pushed him away, arms taut, fists clenched. The air around him buzzed with rage. His eyes grazed Matt's.

"You understand nothing," he said.

"I understand that you're moving in on *her*," said Matt. "Taking advantage."

Valerie felt afraid. She wondered if there was a spare room, a place to get away from Matt.

"It is time for you to leave this house," said Gerard.

* * *

Valerie gazed out the kitchen window. *That reporter on TV looked like you, Gerard. Not as you look now, but as you were, that night in my room long ago.* She looked at the sunlight warming Marguerite's garden, at the fine curtain of time as it opened wide, so that she could see Gerard embracing her child who was not yet born. The *tarte* was fragrant with apples and cinnamon. *Five more minutes and it's done.*

Nothing disappears, she thought.

Through the fog of memory, she heard Matt's voice.

* * *

"Coming, babe?" Sober now, he was stuffing his sneakers in his backpack. When Valerie looked at him, she expected to see a smile that wasn't a smile at all but a hidden knot of arousal and power. Instead she saw that his face was an open window, his fury of the night before clouded by doubt.

"I told you. I'm staying put," she replied.

"You mean for—"

"I'll meet you back home."

"Babe, you can have it done in New York State. Come on."

She glared at him. "I'll have it done here," she said. "Or nowhere."

"Valerie, I love you."

She hesitated. "I'll come home with you if you'll marry me. Otherwise I'll meet you in a week. After my appointment."

"You want a child." He looked stricken with fear.

"Does it help to know I love you?" she asked.

Matt said nothing. He dug his hands into his pockets.

"Valerie — I can't do it," he said.

Why are you so scared, Matt?

He pulled out his keys and tossed them on the table. "Car's yours for when you come home," he said. His face was dark with grief.

"Matt — I don't know when I'm coming home."

He hesitated, then picked up the keys and stuffed them in his pocket.

"I'll see you, Matt."

34

JUST AS SHE WAS about to take the *tarte* out of the oven, Valerie heard Marguerite coming downstairs, making her way into the kitchen.

"No peeking," she said.

"You are forcing me to watch TV." Marguerite rolled her eyes.

"You can go outside and watch the flowers grow. It's nicer."

Marguerite went out into the garden and sat facing the herb bed, her back to the kitchen window. Valerie had meant it as a joke, but the gesture touched her. She took the *tarte* out of the oven, glancing at the TV screen, filthy grey with the haze of New York City's dust and smoke, and she recalled how when she was a kid, the picture would grow fuzzy if the antenna were off-balance. Her sister Karen used to look at the dots and squiggles and say, *Use your imagination. You could be seeing anything at all.*

A few minutes later, Marguerite came back inside. She was holding a clump of cosmos, their petals pink, their centres dabbed with yellow. She put the flowers in a glass of water and set them on the windowsill.

Poor cheerful little things, thought Valerie.

"As you can see," said Marguerite, "the plants are still growing out there."

Valerie was gazing at the TV screen. "When we were kids," she said, "sometimes you'd get nothing but fuzz."

"*Je ne comprends pas.*"

"The screen. Those black and white dots. We used to make up faces. We used to pretend."

"But you have not heard anything more of—"

"Andre?"

"*Oui.*" Marguerite looked troubled. *Who did you think?* her look said.

"He's out there somewhere," Valerie whispered.

* * *

Down from the sky floats the white ash of the dead. Thirty years old, Andre was wandering, dazed and lost in New York City, lost because he no longer knew his way around streets entangled with darkness, with tolling bells, with "the sign that the Cross makes on the world," as James said once.

For certain, this was happening.

Ash in his hair, on his skin and clothes, he was searching for his friend, a good man who loved God. Poor Andre, who doesn't even know whose son he is.

III.

35

MARGUERITE AND ROBERT were about to leave for Laurent Sarazin's wake. They told Valerie they'd meet her at Lisette's.

"Will you invite your friend tonight?" asked Marguerite.

Valerie didn't think so. He'd pick her up afterwards, she said. So they could share their news, if any.

"But you will relax with us."

Valerie said she wouldn't miss the party.

"*Cendrillon* puts down her broom, *bravo*."

"But first I'll do the dishes."

"The dishes, the floors, the walls. I don't want to see you do another thing."

"I'll have to iron my dress." Valerie paused. "Do you have any ironing—"

"*Non, non, non, non.*" Marguerite embraced her. "There's nothing that needs ironing, *ma pauvre. Non.*"

* * *

After they'd left, Valerie set up the iron, then found the tablecloth Lisette had wanted, along with her own dress. Andre was still drifting through her mind, wandering, dazed and lost, trying to find James. *Poor soul.* There was steam coming out of the iron. It was a brand-new one, the kind that shut itself off if you daydreamed too long. Her son had sent her an email. He'd seen the first explosion, and then he picked up the phone and called James. Or maybe it was James who'd called her son who was watching the catastrophic drama from the relative safety of the second tower because he knew that Andre would talk to him in that calm and encouraging voice of his, the mellow voice that had sung in her stairwell, strumming her guitar. Valerie spread the tablecloth on the ironing board, pressing her thoughts into the creases in the linen. She wasn't sure she wanted to know what had happened to Andre. *Look at this handiwork.* Marguerite's embroidery was exquisite. She'd edged the fabric with a delicate vine, a pattern of blue and yellow flowers. What a joy it was to iron it, to admire her eye for beauty, her steady hand at work.

Andre and James. They love each other, those two, she thought. *Andre would have stayed with James.*

No.

Andre would have fled.

Her dress was easier to iron than the tablecloth. It was one of those cotton-polyester things that you roll up and stuff in a suitcase. *Andre, you can't wear that shirt,* she'd say to her son. *Not with all those wrinkles,* but now she's the one doing business in sloppy jeans and mud-caked boots, while he's attired in pressed slacks, sports jackets, crisp, ironed shirts. He wanted to make it big in New York. *My mom's a New Yorker,* he'd tell his friends, and she'd remember the tug of this deepest of connections, her body's grip on a struggling fistful of life.

"I'm going to have the child," she'd said to Rita, having decided to cancel the abortion. Rita looked puzzled. "You came all this way. And you never really.... " Her voice trailed off.

"It was Matt's idea, not mine."

"And he's high-tailing it to Vietnam. He may never come back. They'll lock you up in a home for wayward girls."

"Let them try," Valerie answered.

"You're going to raise it alone?"

Rita had a poster in her bedroom. It was black, and on it was a white female symbol, a cross and circle emblazoned with a red fist. In large white letters, it read CONTROL OF OUR BODIES, CONTROL OF OUR MINDS.

"Just remember, we're here to help," she said.

"Matt may change his mind," said Valerie, but hope died with her words.

Valerie unplugged the iron and put the dress back on its hanger. It was a summery thing, gauzy and light. *I'll need a jacket,* she thought. The air would grow cooler as night fell.

36

ONLY IN THE MOST general terms had Valerie written to Matt about her children. He knew she had two kids. No mention of boys or girls, let alone ages and birthdays. She'd never forgotten his look of grief the day he'd left Toronto, the renunciation she saw in his eyes, the knowledge that he was abandoning his child. *I'll see you, Matt,* she'd replied, but once having said it, she knew she never would.

* * *

She'd promised herself not to worry about Matthew. Yet worry was quicksand, it swallowed everything, Matt along with Andre and James. What if he were on the plane this morning? He would have had no son to call. No one to say goodbye to.

No, but he had his sister in L.A. He had me.

Matt would have called no one. He would have been terrified by flashing lights, by a swollen moon that took up half the sky.

For years he'd tried to forget his time in Vietnam. He'd prayed for the grace to get off drugs, to live without a past, to disassemble with great care the coiled wires and the fuse of time. He'd had to become a priest, to live apart. He'd feared one memory, one single moment pressing on a nerve, its bullet lodged too close to the heart. It made him afraid to move.

* * *

Perhaps that long-ago day of their parting collapsed into this morning when a doomed plane veered over the city with its cargo of terrified human beings, with desperate people on their cell phones, frantic to speak to their loved ones for the last time, and Matt's staring in horror at a flight attendant lying in the aisle with her throat slit. He's about to die in humiliation, shitting his pants as the plane makes its last, lopsided bank before it smashes into the tower.

How could anyone know what might have followed? What might have gone on in Matt's mind, had he been on that plane? Now and again he's hinted at the thing he'd regret until he died. In flight today, he would have wanted to be high on heroin or LSD so he'd die feeling nothing. Only he'd realize that his eternity would be the last dreadful second when his veins were lit up like a shimmering trail through the jungle, when he was loaded up on junk that could kill him quick as a sniper, and he wouldn't care.

If there were an afterlife, he'd spend it going backwards, rifle at hand, stalking the dazzle of the war, seeing the darkness bright with imagined eyes and flashing bayonets and panic. In front of him was a moon as huge as the earth, the light of it gleaming on mangrove leaves, on the blurred shape of a man's body, a soldier bathing behind a palm frond, slats of light and darkness rippling over him. It was night and very late, and the bathing soldier turned around, his face as enormous as that moon, the milky light of it gleaming, and for certain it was a mirage, an enemy trick. He was speaking Vietnamese; no, French. Matt couldn't move, the lit veins of his body were high-voltage wires, and he was burning. The man was going to kill him, this man painted white with dread like a false dawn. It was a trick, this fake grunt turning toward him, saying Matt, Jesus, *and Matt was fucking out of his mind wondering how the hell this wet, naked gook knew his name.*

The scared phony was a coward. He put his hands up, but Matt started screaming, gripping his rifle, running toward the whiteness, taking aim and yelling, Frenchie, I'm gonna kill you *and no one who heard him understood what he meant. Of his victim he remembered only dark hair, frightened eyes, a mouth wide open but no scream, no sound.*

* * *

Matt told me he was in despair, that he'd lost me. He had no idea who he'd killed. The drugs made him lose consciousness before he could turn a weapon on himself. Friendly fire, he wrote to me. That's all it was.

37

THE DOORBELL INTERRUPTED HER reverie. It was Jean-Claude, carrying a bouquet of flowers.

"I am too early, *je suis désolé.*" He looked at Valerie, a gaze full of concern. "You are crying," he said.

She hadn't realized it.

"What is wrong, Valerie?"

"Everything." She dried her eyes.

"You have had news?"

"No," she said. "That's what's wrong."

She thanked him for the flowers — magnificent spikes of pink gladiolas, white calla lilies, crimson anthuriums with broad, green fleshy leaves.

"You are a gardener. I thought these flowers would console you," he said.

She thanked him. "Look at the size. I'll be consoled for life."

"They're blessed," Jean-Claude replied.

"Oh?"

"Only no one goes to church anymore."

"Is that where you bought them?"

"I rescued them from the cathedral."

Lisette's flowers. This is very strange.

The two of them went into the kitchen to find a vase, but there were none large enough. Outside they found a plastic wash-bucket and a garden hose. Jean-Claude filled the bucket with water, and Valerie finished arranging the blooms.

"Have you any news?" she asked.

"Only these flowers."

You could have worse news.

She wondered at the strangeness of ordinary things.

This morning, who would have imagined this?

That's what everyone said about the planes.

* * *

Jean-Claude told her he was having dinner with friends, one of whom owned a seaplane. *I'm going to try to borrow it,* he said. *You know how desperate I am to fly.* After dinner, he'd pick her up at Lisette's. Valerie asked if he'd deliver the tablecloth while she freshened up, so he'd have directions for the evening.

After he left, Valerie stood admiring the extravagant display of flowers, and then she understood that what she wanted right now was as different from this gift as the delicate cluster of lavender in her garden. It was a thing impossible to have, like a dream you struggle to recall and can't. She wanted the moment before Andre disappeared, the moment before Matt ran to catch a plane. She wanted the thing that had brought her to Saint-Pierre, the fragile hope of her marriage, the moment before Gerard began to drift away from her.

38

∞∞

THE TROUBLE BETWEEN THEM began long ago when they were young and in pain, Gerard grieving for Ora, his love for her so real and tangible that she returned to life in a young woman he chanced to meet, a woman pregnant by another man. As for herself, Valerie had wanted Matt's child as much as Ora had wanted Gerard's. Nothing was ever said about this. Ora's spirit was adrift without a body, which is what Valerie understood death to mean. Ora broke into her dreams, trapped inside her until she awoke to her presence. Not just once, but over and over again, and then Matt fled, and then she swore to bear the weight of the thing that Ora was unable to complete.

The night Matt left, Gerard came to her room. "I'm keeping the child," she told him.

"But how?" he asked. "You are alone."

"I'll do it. That's all."

"Dear Valerie." He looked troubled.

"You lost a child," she said.

"But you came here because—"

"And then you brought my child to life."

He embraced her. He asked her to marry him then.

* * *

The times were strange, Valerie understood that. For a short while they lived in Montreal. It happened that she'd loved

173

the haunting melodies of Ora's songs, so that she would have learned them, even if she'd had no connection to her. So she began to play and sing her compositions, adapting the fingerings of the *oud* for the guitar. Something changed with the singing, a part of Valerie shifting away from herself, slipping into a new form in the same way that water takes the shape of a pitcher. A kind of snare, but what relief she felt — her chaotic life held in shape by music, by a stronger spirit than her own.

She and Gerard had just been married, and Valerie felt confused, still hurt from losing Matt. Her mother had been upset when she guessed the reason for her trip to Toronto, then horrified when she learned that Valerie was marrying a man she'd known only a few weeks. It felt as if she'd dreamt that summer, as if she'd woken to find herself facing the results of her own carelessness — pregnant, abandoned by the father; grateful that she'd found a man who loved her, who loved even more the soul into which she'd vanished.

Sometimes in bed, he'd call her Ora, and it was an unspoken thing between them, that she'd let him do this. She'd disappear, drifting into spices, jasmine and pomegranate, as if she were Solomon's bride. She'd remember a country she'd never seen: the waters of Yom Kinneret, the Negev Desert, the fragrance of orange and the taste of black, sweet coffee, the staccato beating of clay drums in the covered market of Jerusalem.

"Take me there," he'd whisper, her name on his lips, on his tongue exploring her mouth.

She and Ora had become one person. It didn't matter what he called her.

Yet Ora was dead, and time overtook her. Valerie's French grew better than hers had been, her voice richer and stronger. The world forgot the disaster that took her life, and after a while, so did Valerie. She and Gerard were married two years when Valerie became pregnant with Chantal. As a mother, she grew in confidence. Her own mother forgave her and welcomed her grandchildren. The memory of Ora drifted away as Valerie returned to herself. She began to realize that Gerard seemed lost.

Little by little, everything changed between them.

* * *

It's because of genocide, Valerie thought when Gerard stopped saying much. *It's about what you suffered in your youth,* she'd realize when he became obsessed with injustice. Then he began losing interest in sex, and she became suspicious.

Because the towers fell, she thought now, *would that make it right for me to sleep with Jean-Claude?* Perhaps it would have consoled the man, yet he didn't take advantage of her state of mind, didn't make real her imagined world where she'd fly beyond time with him, away from sorrow and memory. Imagination was one thing; action was another. She felt close to Jean-Claude who, even in his suffering, was trying to console her. She imagined that pain had seared away the superficial dross of his life, leaving behind the pure ore of compassion. She once thought this was true of Gerard, but after what he'd done to their marriage, she was no longer sure.

* * *

Valerie remembered 1994, when Gerard returned from Rwanda shadowed by death, as hesitant in his own home as a tourist in an unfamiliar city. She watched as he stared in disbelief at a fresh bar of soap, at the rush of hot water from the shower, at the crispness of a clean shirt as he dressed, as if her taking the time to iron it were unthinkable, as if he couldn't register domesticity while holding in his mind some ravaged life, some poor bloodied dress or pair of pants. It was one or the other — civilization or savagery — his soul could not accommodate them both, and it was savagery he'd witnessed, madness to clothe these memories in a fresh shirt and tailored slacks.

He went for a walk, came back, gulped down a double scotch.

"I don't want to talk," he said. "Not now."

"When you're ready."

"There is no such thing as 'ready,'" he said.

His face was a ruin. His eyes held the gutted reflection of a place he'd never be ready to talk about, because "ready" belonged to a world of logic, of understanding, of finding words for the truth. Valerie felt helpless. She took his hand between hers and held it.

"Don't love me," he said.

"But why shouldn't I love you?"

"I can't get this world off my skin. This filth."

"You are not obliged to smear yourself in shit!" she yelled.

"Forgive me, Valerie," he said at last. In bed, he wore a condom.

"Don't take me for a fool," she said.

"Why do you love me, then?"

"To prove it can be done."

She wanted him to make up for what he had stolen from her.

They made love, dissolving into his nightmare haze of scotch and panicky sex and gunfire, and he drew her into such a terrible place that she could see the horror and butchery that he had seen, so that afterwards she wept and said, "Gerard, you have to stop the work you do. You'll lose your mind."

Only that night was her mistake, the way that trying heroin is a mistake. After that, she wanted this lost man — the one the journalist kept hidden — because on his tongue and on his lips was the same man who'd come to her room so long ago to hear her sing, who'd caressed her and the vague echo of a dead woman's presence, who'd breathed a soul into her unborn child. She had to go back there. She had to find the fork in the road that set him walking toward the vale of the dead, afraid all the while that she was that fork, that Ora's death had come to life in her, that she had caused him to suffer.

"No, that is not true," said Gerard.

"Than what is?"

"That I am obsessed. I don't know why I hurt you, Valerie."

They made love again. She followed him into the darkness, then brought him home.

Their lives changed. He was afraid so often.

"I can't," he'd say in his sleep. "I can't."

After Rwanda, he drifted away from her, returning from his assignments like a soldier on leave, in need of a woman. He'd pour her a drink, he'd want comfort for a night or two. As strange as it seemed, it felt to her like new love, as if she were having an affair with her own husband.

Yet just as often, he'd return, a stranger with no interest in her, who wanted to sleep alone. He was away more often than not. Uncertain of what to do, Valerie attended to her small business and hoped the situation might resolve itself. In the year of the new millennium, they would celebrate thirty years of marriage.

* * *

Andre and James were coming up for the occasion. *We're going to cook something special for you guys,* said Andre's email. *James' recipe: lobster on a bed of white clam risotto.* They'd already had to postpone the dinner a month because Gerard had been in Jerusalem, covering the rumblings of Intifada Round Two. This time he was delayed because he'd left for Cairo, flying from there to the port of Aden, Yemen, where suicide bombers had just attacked the U.S.S. *Cole.*

"Why do you need to be there?" asked Valerie when he called.

"Because seventeen sailors were killed," he said.

Afterwards he had trouble booking a flight back. He called again and told them to start the dinner without him.

James seated them at the table and took their hands. "Let us give thanks for the grace of our friendship," he said.

In the middle of the first course, Andre slammed down his fork. "You're not pissed off?" he asked James.

"At what?"

"My dad being a no-show."

"At least he called," said James.

"Too bad he doesn't realize it's work to cook all this."

"Cooking's what I enjoy doing most," said James. "It isn't work. Being pissed off is work."

Valerie asked James where his culinary gifts came from.

"God," he said.

"Not your mother?"

"I've taken a vow," said James. "Not to pass on what I received at home."

"Sour grapes?" asked Andre. "Rotten apples?"

"Nothing you're allowed to send through the mail," said James, and he laughed.

* * *

When Gerard returned from Yemen, he dropped his suitcase, looked at Valerie and said, "I'm sorry, I know, I should not have done this, but you have no idea how dangerous—"

"Andre was so disappointed," she said.

"It's a new thing in the world, this kind of terror."

"There's nothing new about people getting killed."

"But Valerie—"

"You weren't even on assignment there. You were chasing trouble."

"No, this is different. This violence is about religion."

"How different is that? 'It's about Marxism. Or Maoism.' Violence is always 'about' some crazy thing."

"The world needs to know about it," he said.

"Says you, big ego. The world doesn't give a shit."

He paused. "So, I should forget it. Tend my garden, with you and Voltaire."

"Andre and James put a meal on the table," she said. "You waited until the last minute to call."

He walked away.

* * *

Gerard worked hard on his investigation, but his TV report on the *Cole* bombing and the role of extremist groups in the Middle East wasn't as well received as his probings into food shortages and ethnic cleansing had been. *Les américains l'ont mérité*, they had it coming, said some of his colleagues who shrugged the whole thing off. They saw nothing peculiar about the motives of the attackers, arguing that in the end, radicalism was about politics, not faith. They pointed out that if you looked at church attendance in Quebec or France or even Canada — and if you were at all astute — you might just notice that modernity was killing off religion.

* * *

Gerard came and went. In August, he took Valerie's hands in his and kissed them and asked her forgiveness for his indifference. He invited her to New York — as if the two of them were lovers, cheating on the marriage they once had.

"I am going to be in Saint-Pierre," said Valerie.

He looked dismayed. "Alone?"

"As you've been," she said. " All these years."

"*C'est vrai.*" It's true.

"I'm there for the flora," she told him. "And to think about us, Gerard."

"Yes," he said. "I understand."

He reached out to hold her, but she'd left the room by then.

39

JEAN-CLAUDE RETURNED from his errand. He looked bemused.
"Lisette was frantic," he said.

"*Porquoi?*"

"This evening was to be *festive*, she tells me."

"She doesn't think Marguerite will be surprised?"

"It seems Marguerite is coming from a wake. Along with everyone else."

"That can't be helped."

"The poor man," he said. "His poor family."

"Don't be too hard on Lisette. She was fond of Laurent Sarazin."

"And you know this?" he asked.

"Those were her flowers you pinched from the cathedral."

Jean-Claude became silent. "I was foolish. I must return them."

"Of course."

"How sad everything is," he said at last. "The bell is still tolling. Listen."

* * *

When they left the *pension*, it was late afternoon, and through her eyes, Saint-Pierre had lost none of its morning strangeness. Streets appeared to list seaward like doomed ships, each frame building pressing hard against the next as if in an effort to remain standing. Valerie couldn't grasp the distance between blocks, how long it might take her to cross the street.

"I must be tired," she said. "I can't see depth."

"I can," Jean-Claude replied. He offered her his arm. "At least I think I can."

"Either you can or you can't." *You must be tired, too,* she thought.

"I don't know which it is," he said. "Just because I see it doesn't mean it's there."

Valerie wondered if she'd ever again have a sane conversation with anyone.

When they reached Rue Albert Briand, they stood across the street from the *Fromagerie Leduc* — where the yellow house had been. "It's *gone*," she said.

"No. We are looking at it."

Jean-Claude was right. The yellow clapboard house stood between the dress shop and the travel agency, but its colour had faded in the afternoon light. The green planter was still there, with its flush of pink geraniums. The lace curtains were pulled shut. On the front lawn was a placard. *En Vente/À Louer,* it read. *For sale/For rent.* Beside the front door, Valerie saw the dark outline of a square, as if a sign had been pried loose.

"The tile," she said. "The exclamation point."

"We must be on the wrong street," said Jean-Claude.

They circled the block, then returned to Rue Albert Briand. Valerie went into the dress shop and asked the clerk if she knew about the café.

"That odd little place?"

"It's such a charming—"

"It comes and goes," she said.

"We were just here at noontime."

She looked at them, puzzled. "Maybe someone has bought the house at last."

* * *

"We must have been mistaken," said Jean-Claude.

"Some mistake. I checked my email here. My son—"

"Yes, I understand." His voice trailed off.

"Your brother—"

"I also checked—"

As if he could tell her anything. As if he had power over time, as if he'd managed quite by accident to punch in the wrong year when he asked her out for coffee. Jean-Claude looked weary. "Perhaps we've shuffled time," he said. "A great poker game."

"The cards all out of order."

"We are trapped," he said.

* * *

They walked over to the café at the Place du Général de Gaulle. Once they were seated, Valerie noticed Jean-Claude glancing at her arm. He reached out and touched her silver bracelet.

"How beautiful. Where did you get this?"

"It belonged to my husband's fiancée. She died young."

"*C'est triste.*"

"He never got over it." She told him the story of Ora.

He withdrew his hand. For a moment, he said nothing.

"She belongs to this day," he said at last.

"It's true. Yes." She paused. "As if time never was. As if her plane went up in smoke this morning."

"*Oui. Je comprends.*"

"Thank you. Almost no one understands this."

"Your husband must. It is fortunate that he found you. After his loss."

Unsure how much to tell him, Valerie was silent. "I came here to think about us," she said at last. "And then, this morning—"

Afraid of a rockslide of terror, she took a deep breath as she looked out over the water, at the soft clouds, the lazy sailboats drifting by. Ora, she thought, had been woven into the fabric of injustice, of every disgraceful thing that Gerard had set out to expose, and this transformation was, in a sense, her second death. Perhaps she, Valerie, had also died for him. For a while Gerard would lose interest in her, and then passion would hiss and spark, as it did after his return from Rwanda. Then he'd go overseas again, coming back for a couple of illicit nights, dangerous encounters, whatever their imaginations chose to name them. Or he'd go on assignment and vanish. He'd return preoccupied. He wouldn't touch her. In a day or two he'd leave again.

And now he was one of those anguished souls in Manhattan. And this time, it was she who'd fled.

* * *

"I have heard nothing more from my son," she said.

"Nor I, of my brother. My sister-in-law is checking all the hospitals."

"Many people have fled by boat," she said. "Andre could be with them."

"I hope it does not sound trivial," he replied. "But the waters of New York are calm. A good day for such a trip."

Valerie agreed. She imagined Andre making a dash to the ferry, and then she pictured Battery Park, a lazy afternoon, she, Gerard and the kids on the boat, circling the Statue of Liberty. She loved the calm of this time of year. Summer (even late summer in the North Atlantic) didn't lend itself to a crisis. The season was too languid, too sensual, sailboats drifting in the harbour; the froth on a chill beer, the warmth right down to the bones that says *be well*. Fear and Dread had to stand in line for a café table like everyone else, *c'est tout*. On a day like this, it was possible to hope. Yet she'd been fooled before.

"Have you ever had a difficult flight?" she asked him.

"Once or twice we've had to turn back to Orly because of engine trouble," he said.

"And nothing else?"

He paused. "I once flew into the desert."

"And something went wrong?"

"It *was* wrong." He paused. "I was going to leave my family. I changed my mind."

"Did you ever regret it?" she asked.

"Changing my mind? No. I was not home often enough to regret it."

His children had left home. His wife had since passed away.

She told him about Mr. Groves' plane and the odd stories surrounding its disappearance, remembering that hot June day on the airfield, the kids picnicking while the adults fretted. *The grownups will take care of everything,* said the tart fizzle of Aunt Ann's lemonade. They'd find Mr. Groves. Things would work out somehow. They didn't.

She'd never quite got over the fact that they didn't.

He listened.

* * *

"When I first saw you, I knew you were a pilot," she said.

"But how?"

"You seemed caught up in the sky somehow. For a moment I thought you might be Mr. Groves, returned at last. A messenger."

"I would like to take you flying, if I could," he said.

"Would it help me find my son?"

"It would help you find hope." He hesitated. "Perhaps we will find what Mr. Groves was looking for."

* * *

Jean-Claude offered to lend her his laptop so that she could check for news, and so they left the square, heading toward his flat on Rue Normand, near the Place de La Cathédrale. They walked through a narrow, cobbled laneway that opened out into the deserted street. There was no one to see them in the shadows. They might have been the last two people on earth.

Dust. She floated into the sky, disembodied.

They walked through the laneway, along Rue Normand.

The bell was still tolling. It marked no hour, only unremitting grief.

* * *

He was drawn to her, she knew that. For sure, he would have taken her to bed, if she'd let him. Two lonely, frightened people, both wanting solace, stopping by his flat. No, she was too distressed for love.

She took his laptop. "You're very kind," she told him, and she wept.

There was no one here to see her. Only him.

"*Je comprends,*" he said, and he put an arm around her.

"Poor Andre." Her body could feel the weight of him, as if he were still unborn.

He held her and let her cry.

40

JEAN-CLAUDE CALLED A TAXI, and together they went back to the *pension*. It was still difficult to call New York, he told her. As for himself, he could go to his airline office and use the computer there. Later he'd meet her at Lisette's.

Valerie felt relief, even comfort. She could not give up hope so soon. She had, at least, found friendship, and she felt grateful that she didn't have to burden Marguerite and Robert with the full weight of her anguish. She worried that there might be more attacks. Jean-Claude had reminded her that in their parents' time, war had come close to these remote and lonely islands. When the Nazis occupied France, they'd used Saint-Pierre as a listening post. *Nazi ears, spying on North America* — Robert or Marguerite had used that phrase. In some new form, it could happen again.

Nothing was safe — not then, not now.

* * *

The *pension* was quiet. Marguerite had left the kitchen TV on, humming away like a household appliance, a mini-refrigerator that kept the news nice and fresh. Valerie looked, imagining she might see Gerard, ghost-white and silent, and she fixed on a reporter in the crowd, a man with a mike in his hand, his hand on someone's arm, on a woman's sleeve thick with ash, and then the reporter put his arm around the woman, and then he put his mouth on hers, and then he vanished into whiteness.

Valerie felt a slow awareness rising over the brim of fear.

As if she were watching Gerard. Or herself.

Seduced like that, pulled in.

* * *

She set up Jean-Claude's computer, logged on and waited for the internet connection to plunk out its four-note welcome while the late-day sun idled on the brilliant purple of the coleus leaves, the golden trumpet-flower in a glass bowl on the windowsill, the wonder that in this catastrophic world, the day could offer its own small gifts.

In her inbox was an email from Gerard. He'd sent it an hour ago — four-thirty, New York time. The subject line read *Valerie*. Clicking it open, she saw that it was blank. From time to time he'd send her blanks when he was on assignment, when he was too frazzled to articulate a thought. It was his way of letting her know he was safe.

She wondered where he'd sent it from. *He's at Andre's place. Gerard's with Andre. I have to talk to my son.* She dialled his number.

"Hello," said a man's voice.

What luck. She'd gotten through. "Andre?"

"I'm his neighbour, Ian," said the man. "I'm here to water the plants."

Andre must have closed the windows when he left for work, Ian said, and he'd turned the air conditioner off, too, but the entire city was covered with a haze of smoke and dust and the stench was leaking in through the cracks.

"Plants get stressed in times of chaos," he said. "I firmly believe that."

Valerie explained that gardening was her profession.

"Andre has your green thumb," said Ian.

"I think I might have seen him on TV. Earlier today."

"Honestly, Mrs. Lefèvre, I hope you're right."

She asked Ian to call her if he had news.

"You know, someone left Andre's computer on," he said. "That's so not him."

Maybe Andre came home, she thought, *then ran out again. He'd checked his email, hoping for news about James, and he was so distracted by worry that he forgot to turn his computer off. Then in came Gerard.*

Ian didn't think so.

"One of them would have looked after the plants," he insisted.

***

Valerie was half-inclined to believe Ian, knowing it was just as likely that Gerard might have found a computer in a newsroom or a cyber-café. Or maybe he was carrying his laptop — she hadn't thought of that. She stared at the blank screen. As she did, it sounded two notes and the red mailbox flag went up. She clicked it open. *Can't call you, phones are down,* Gerard wrote. *I will not rest until I understand what has happened here.*

My heart is with our beloved sons.

***

She read the last sentence again and again. *Beloved sons.* As if long ago when Gerard embraced her unborn child, he'd included the man her son would love.

Other than that, it was one of Gerard's hurry-up emails, a variation of the standard one he always sent from his foreign assignments. *Phones down, very busy, can't rest* — the words spun with a dizzy excitement, a passion for truth that made her feel wrong about asking too many questions.

I will not rest until I understand what has happened here. And here. And here.

Time was melting in the heat.

Gerard is standing too close to the pyre, the one that has never stopped burning. He's pulling Ora from the wreckage, his mouth on hers.

Gerard blessed Andre, before he was born.

All of us vanishing into whiteness.

41

GATHERING HER PARCELS, Valerie locked up the *pension* and began her walk to Lisette's. Twilight was falling in the garden, on neighbourhoods silent with unease, on TVs glowing in the windows. No one was out in the street. Even at rest, Saint-Pierre breathed the worried stillness of the whole earth.

She turned her cell phone on.

Marguerite and Robert lived at the base of the hill, its stash of houses clinging to the slope like tough vegetation, roots sinking into hard soil. Lisette's house was near the end of a road that twisted upwards, on a little street jammed with motorbikes, tiny row houses, thumbprint gardens ragged with clover and bergamot, front doors that opened on to the narrow sidewalk. The neighbourhood had the offhand charm of a Norman village, its cobblestones lustrous, as if they'd been washed by the sea.

Lisette's house had a bright red door and a tiny stoop crowded with pots of straggly pink geraniums. Beyond the door was a long, narrow corridor that led to a flight of stairs. Valerie went upstairs and knocked.

"*Ma chère,* you are early, thank goodness."

Lisette took her parcels, and Valerie could smell the fragrance of her cologne, *Roses Sauvages.* Her black hair gleamed, knife-edge straight, and she wore a long rose-coloured dress, flow-er-shaped earrings, a string of pearls. Her home was stylish, a leafy perch above the town, its glass doors overlooking the bay, opening onto a small terrace garden. To Valerie's eyes, it was a hidden wonder, a vantage-point well-concealed by trees. As she peered through the canopy of green, she saw water, and she recalled Gerard making a video high above Manhattan, its two great rivers conjoined below him.

Yesterday.

Lisette took the *tarte* from her. "Oh, but this is lovely, *ma chère*," she said.

"It was so easy."

"My own *chef-d'oeuvre* is warming in the oven. *Brie aux abricots.*"

"Did I see you in the *fromagerie* today?"

"*Oui*, and so you met Jacques Leduc," said Lisette. "Such a conscientious man, *n'est-ce pas?* He didn't go home to watch TV."

"He has a TV in the shop," Valerie remarked.

"Humming in the background, *c'est tout*. My husband can't take his eyes off the screen."

"*Oui. Je comprends.*"

"You'd think the sky was falling down."

* * *

Lisette had invited twelve friends, but Laurent Sarazin's sudden demise (along with his wife's absence) had reduced that number to ten.

"We'll have leftovers," she said.

"I'm sorry about your loss."

Lisette paused. "*Merci*. A dear man," she said.

"Did he love flowers?"

"Why yes, he did." Lisette looked startled by the question.

"I saw you carrying flowers to the church. That's why I asked."

"*Ce sont pour les obsèques,*" said Lisette. "For the funeral."

And Jean-Claude swiped them, Valerie thought. She felt

uneasy. There was some connection between those grandiose flowers and the day's horror and how Lisette had carried those blooms through the streets of Saint-Pierre, broadcasting her private grief to a world in shock. *I loved him, I loved him, doesn't that count for anything?* Now Lisette was crying like a child, dabbing at her eyes with a handkerchief, unconcerned that she'd smeared her eye shadow, because Laurent Sarazin had made her weep, a kind man who'd no doubt given Lisette more than one bouquet of flowers. *Thank you for your business,* he'd say, if others were in earshot. Or *we value our customers. Bon anniversaire,* as his hand brushed hers.

Each of his bouquets would have been tidy and compact, perhaps an arrangement of carnations and forget-me-nots delivered at a precise time, on a particular day; a vast accumulation of restrained loveliness over the years, acknowledged by the explosion of grief in Lisette's garish funeral offering. *Sitting in a bucket in Marguerite's garden,* Valerie thought.

This was no day to cause anyone grief. She hoped Jean-Claude was as good as his word, that he'd return the flowers to the church.

No wonder she didn't go to the wake, poor soul, thought Valerie. *She would have fallen apart.* Lisette ran off to wash her face, and moments later, she returned, her makeup re-applied. She was calm, as if nothing had happened.

* * *

Guests started to arrive, beginning with Jacques Leduc and his wife. The owner of the *fromagerie* greeted Valerie, and she was about to thank him, that she'd managed to check her email, that she'd taken his advice and asked at the pottery shop, but she stopped herself. Too complicated — she'd have to mention that strange woman who'd sent her to a café that later vanished.

"Have you had a chance to try the *fromage* St. Paulin?" he asked.

With pleasure, she told him how tasty it was.

His wife apologized to Valerie, that she hadn't been at the shop to assist her. More guests arrived, including the couple from the bakery who'd supplied Robert with breakfast croissants that morning. Valerie realized she'd seen the wife at the cathedral when she noticed the lace collar on her blouse.

"Weren't you in the group at the church?" the woman asked her.

Valerie explained that she'd come upon it by accident.

Madame Leduc had been there also.

So were Andre and James, Valerie thought. *You were holding hands with them.* She felt comforted, that the two women were keeping her son and his partner alive.

* * *

Lisette's husband Pierre was the manager of *Banque des Isles.* He was a careful man, soft-spoken, discreet in dress and language, as suited the financial confidant of half the businesses in town. He'd come inside to join the guests with cordial handshakes, greeting them with the modulated tones of a *présentateur* on Radio-France. With him was a sombre-looking gendarme in uniform, dark and with a trim moustache, his flat-topped *képi* in hand. The sight of him rattled Valerie, as if he'd come with dreadful news.

"My brother," said Pierre.

Valerie recalled that Marguerite had mentioned him. The young man had just arrived from France for a two-year posting, she'd said. *It is not like Canada. Here when the policeman takes a break, it is not with coffee and* beignets. *A glass of brandy,* un morceau de gâteau ... *he's a charming man and company for Lisette.*

The gendarme, like his brother, looked too serious to fool around with another man's wife. He'd come here straight from work, he said, and he'd have an added shift tonight.

"That is unfortunate," said Pierre.

His brother shrugged. "They need me at the airport. *En cas d'urgence.*"

"An emergency? In Saint-Pierre?"

"Well—"

42

T HERE WAS A TAP at the door and Lisette flung it open. Robert stepped inside, then Marguerite. She looked around at everyone, perplexed.

"*Mes amis*, you were just at the wake," she said.

"The wake is over," said Lisette.

"*Bon anniversaire*," said the guests, but not in unison, as their host would have preferred.

Lisette invited them into the living room, and her husband poured champagne while she and Valerie served *hors d'oeuvres*. The guests sipped and nibbled, their voices soft, their words intent, as if resuming a conversation that had just been interrupted.

"There could be a bombing campaign," said the gendarme.

The other men nodded, listening.

"May I have your attention?" asked Lisette.

The room, already quiet, grew silent.

"We don't drink champagne in the funeral home. The wake is over and Marguerite is celebrating sixty-five years of life. A toast!"

"*Bon anniversaire!*" Everyone raised their glasses. Moments later, they resumed their conversation.

"War would be justified," someone remarked.

"Before we do that," said another, "let us honour the dead."

"Us?" asked a third voice.

"Yes, us," came the answer. "The *attentat* was meant for all of us."

Lisette and Valerie went into the kitchen, took the *brie aux abricots* out of the oven and brought it into the living room.

"You must try this, everyone," said Lisette.

"The poor Sarazin kids," the women murmured to each other. "They took it so hard."

Jacques Leduc dug into the cheese he'd sold that morning. "*Bien fait,*" he said to Lisette. He grinned at her, then helped himself to more.

Valerie was thinking about Andre.

Lisette sat down beside her, took a chunk of bread, scooped up some of the melted brie and handed it to her. "You must taste it," she said.

Valerie took the morsel. "*C'est délicieux,*" she answered.

"Flying will not be fun anymore," someone said.

"If you ask me, it's a plot," came the reply.

"You people — you are so absorbed in politics, I'll end up eating it all myself," said Lisette.

"It's delicious, *ma chère,*" said Marguerite.

Lisette's husband poured the rest of the champagne. The window was open, and the sounds of the street and the town below were drifting in on the breeze.

"That damn bell is still tolling," said Lisette.

***

They sat down to a light dinner — *charcuterie, salade, pâtés, fromages,* a selection of wines. There were candles on the table, two beautiful tapers. In the lengthening shadows, the room seemed to grow smaller, a tree-hollow full of skittish creatures, their fearful gazes turned on the night.

Lisette's husband turned to Valerie. "You are from New York," he said.

197

She felt like an immigrant with a tubercular cough, about to be deported. "I was born there," she told him.

"Your family is safe?" he asked.

Valerie wasn't sure what to say. "I've heard from my husband," she said. "He's trying to locate our son."

Everyone grew silent. Valerie felt as if they were watching her, a foreigner who both fascinated and stunned them. No *saint-pierrais* ever got this close to the breath of fire crackling in the world. She could sense how tantalized they were by a *new-yorkaise*, yet at the same time afraid, as if she would crumble into poisonous ash and infect them, too.

"Such a shock," said Pierre.

"No one's ever heard of these *kamikazes*," said Robert.

"Ah, and you were sure it was an accident," said Marguerite.

"But so was I," said Lisette. "Who on earth would *think...?*"

Valerie got up and began to clear the table. Lisette helped her.

The gendarme sat, his hands folded over his *kepi*, looking sombre, saying nothing. *He's in uniform,* Valerie thought. *On the job. Maybe it would be improper for him to venture an opinion.* His steady gaze unnerved her, as if he knew more than he was saying.

"Now you mustn't eat and run," Pierre chided him.

The officer glanced at his watch.

Lisette found a candle for the *tarte*. Everyone wished Marguerite a happy birthday as she cut the first slice.

"*C'est parfait,*" she said. "My *tartes* are never as lovely."

"You have made the crust with how much butter?" asked the baker.

With secret ingredients, thought Valerie. *A pinch of memory. A kilo of dread.* She promised to write out the recipe.

"It calls for a toast, this *tarte*," said Lisette.

"*Mais oui,*" said Marguerite. "Valerie has made the day sweet."

With great solemnity, they drank to her.

After dessert, the men left the room to watch TV. Valerie gave her gift to Marguerite, who lifted the box and smiled. "You can't fool me," she said. "I know what it is."

"Rocks," said Valerie. "Seashells."

"You bought it where?"

Valerie hesitated. "*L'Usine de la Paix*. I think."

"That store has been closed for months," said Marguerite.

"Maybe some other."

"I know all the pottery shops in town. That one went out of business."

Marguerite was so vehement that Valerie thought she'd offended her.

"I picked up their business card at the *fromagerie*," she said.

"*There is no one at that address,*" Marguerite insisted. "I tell you, I drove by only yesterday. The store's boarded up."

"Never mind where I bought it."

"I'm so sorry, *ma chère*," said Marguerite. "I'm getting carried away."

She unwrapped the gift, and from the tissue paper, she removed the blue-black vessel with its shimmering glaze, its rings tapering into a neck as graceful as a swan's.

"Alive," said Marguerite. "*C'est extraordinaire.*"

"*Mon Dieu*, it glows in the dark," said Lisette.

Marguerite turned the pot around, gazing at it with a practiced eye. "This potter is a genius," she said.

I am sure it was Gerard's, the most beautiful object in his room. It shone with incandescent fire. Ora's dead, he told me.

At that moment, Valerie saw a shadow. Silent as a cat, the gendarme moved through the hallway to the stairs, his *kepi* on his head, his back straight. He seemed in a hurry, anxious to disappear.

43

VALERIE'S CELL PHONE RANG. She excused herself and stepped out on to the terrace. Jean-Claude was calling to tell her he was on his way.

"Have you heard from your husband?" he asked.

She mentioned the email.

"*Mon amie*, I've found us a sea-plane."

"I'll look forward to that," she said.

"I just have to be in the sky."

Valerie took a deep breath. "Have you had any news of your brother?"

"*Non*," said Jean-Claude. His voice broke. "I have not."

* * *

Valerie came inside. She'd decided to join the men in the TV room.

Lisette glanced at the cell phone in her hand. "Is everything all right?" she asked.

"That's what I need to find out."

Marguerite got up and followed Valerie.

"This is no way to spend a birthday," Lisette sighed. "What's done is done."

The TV room was as silent as church. On the screen was a park in New York City. It was shrouded in flags and banners, filled with hundreds of grieving souls. Everything shuddered in candlelight. Valerie remembered the stone steps, the statue of George Washington on horseback.

"It's Union Square," she said.

As if that means a thing to anyone.

Squat vigil lights crowded the steps on the south side of the square, waxy stubs as thick and bruised as thumbs crushed under hammers. Their flames were quavering in the breeze, casting light on flowers and crucifixes, statues of the Buddha, people burning incense. As she watched, Valerie felt excised from her surroundings, as if an invisible trowel had pried her loose, shallow root and tender branch. She wanted to be planted in this soil of human nourishment. More than this, she wanted to dissolve into the crowd of mourners, to be the wind passing through the image on the screen of a tall redheaded man in a dark raincoat, his arm around a fair man with a sports jacket and a laptop.

Andre, James. If I were wind, I could touch you.

Nausea came rushing in at high tide. Valerie excused herself. She wanted air.

"Are you finding this hard, *ma chère?*" asked Marguerite.

She didn't answer. *Alive.* Yet the sight of the two men had made her feel ill.

She doesn't like to let on, whispered Marguerite to her sister.

Valerie felt for her cell phone, then ran out the door.

44

D OWN THE LONG FLIGHT of stairs Valerie ran — through the corridor and out the front door, down a spiralled street that felt as coiled and tense as a rattler. She ran right to the bottom of the hill, as if danger had lit a match to her clothing, as if she meant to jump into the sea.

She'd seen Andre — twice today, on TV. Three times (if you counted apparitions). Only this time she'd seen something else.

Calm down. If it were anything to concern you, Gerard would have called.

Gerard had her cell phone number and he'd jotted down the number of the *pension*. Her husband had beautiful, neat handwriting. When the kids were small, he'd sometimes take them to his TV studio. Andre and Chantal would admire his big, block letters, how he'd write their names in red felt marker on his story-board. On weekends, he'd play a game with them. He'd write down a word or phrase in French and get the kids to translate. One point for each correct word, three points for a phrase.

For example: *Meilleurs Amis — Best Friends.*

Gerard's handwriting. That poster on TV, in Union Square.

* * *

She made her way down the hill. It was a cool evening, but at this moment the sky was clear and dark, and the waning moon had not yet risen. Stars were alight and the Dipper was turning in its slow, majestic circle around the North Star, sublime and indifferent to the world. In Manhattan, the sky was grey, foul with smoke. In Saint Pierre she had, at least, the blessing of the stars.

Her sister Karen told her once that the stars had Arabic names. *Vega, Deneb, Altair, summer stars.* She glanced westward. *A lot of Muslims got killed today,* she thought. *They said it on the news. All kinds of immigrants went missing.* It had to be true — the TV showed bilingual signs in Union Square, people searching for their loved ones in English and Spanish. A few of the posters had Chinese characters, others added Arabic script to English, another sign had Russian letters. French words, too. *There are New Yorkers who speak French, who come from Haiti or Senegal. There would have been more than one French sign. If you were French, you'd write the French words first.*

DISPARU — *MISSING*

The TV showed candles in the square, burning down to bruised stubs, casting light on the flags of all nations. Canada's flag, too — a red Maple Leaf on a white field, neighbour to a miniature Stars and Stripes, the flags of both her countries bound together. *Of what use were countries?* she wondered. *Their boundaries no longer protect you.* Matt had to write a paper once on Karl Marx, who didn't write about countries, only classes — oppressors and oppressed.

All that is solid melts into air.

For a moment, Valerie remembered Matthew — young, before everything happened. Andre bore his father's looks, and it had been her son's youthful face she'd seen on Gerard's poster, alongside the two flags.

All that is holy is profaned.

One of two faces.

DISPARU

* * *

Valerie tried to stay calm, breathing with slow breaths in and out, imagining the roll and glide of the ocean waves, high tide, low tide; the Dipper sweeping around the pole like the hand of a cosmic timepiece. She wondered if time had come to an end, or if once again, she'd slipped backwards into another moment that had vanished long ago. *Matt and those damn clocks,* she thought. *This is all his fault.*

* * *

As she reached the bottom of the hill, she saw Jean-Claude approaching her.

"You have left the party so soon?" he asked.

"I have to go home."

"You're very close to the *pension.*"

"No, I mean *home.* New York City. Andre's alive."

"How do you know that?"

"I just saw him on TV. But then I saw — "

She told him about the *missing* sign in Union Square. She began to weep.

Jean-Claude held her. "If we fly, we will find hope," he said.

"We're not allowed. We'll be shot down."

Jean-Claude drew back from her, then took her hand in both of his. "Do you remember that pilot you told me about?" he asked.

"Mr. Groves. The one who disappeared."

"No, he did not. He found hope in another dimension."

Poor Jean-Claude, she thought. *You're coming unstrung.*

"He'd found an encrypted *système de pilotage,*" he continued. "Left from the Second World War."

"That story's been around so long, it's—"

"Listen," said Jean-Claude. "My father was a pilot and he had friends who were veterans of war who—"

"Took off and disappeared. No one's heard from them since, right?"

"No one found *Monsieur* Groves because they didn't know how to look for him."

"But what are you telling me?" she asked.

"I don't know," he whispered.

"Well—"

"Murderers. They cursed the sky."

"You want to make it whole again."

"Yes."

45

They were close to the *pension*, but they didn't continue eastward. They walked south instead, following the sweep of another dark road bending toward the southwest, engulfing them in a fog-bank, a spray of water. They weren't far from the *barachois* — the inlet sheltering the harbour and separating them from the *pension* and the town. Southward they walked, ahead of them the dim halos of airport lights in the distance, then along another fogbound road that slithered off toward Étang du Cap Noir, the large pond abutting the airport runway. There were scant trees along the pond; the shore rock-strewn. Here and there were coves punched out of the barren landscape, as if the rocky soil were edible and some enormous canine had bitten off a chunk or two. Valerie'd walked along the airport road before, but she'd never bothered to cross the fields, thinking there was little of interest anywhere near the runway.

Now she noticed a small dock protruding into calm water. Two ancient dories were moored there, their red and blue paint peeled and chipped. The boats, she thought, were far too picturesque for the real work of fishing. They looked posed, as if some journalist had arranged them for a photograph, a quaint image for the Travel section of the weekend paper. Only the photographer might have walked away, forgetting to take the picture, leaving it hovering in air. Something had distracted him. Maybe this morning, before the towers were attacked, he'd come here planning to shoot. Or fifty years ago, before the towers were even built, a woman ambled out to the dock with a squat box camera and tripod — who knows. Time ebbed away, lapping against a pair of weathered boats still waiting for the shutter to open, for the camera's lens to press them into light. At the far end of the dock was a seaplane, shimmering white in the darkness. It looked to her like a creature born of longing and desire, not the product of a factory floor, of a riveter's careful work.

"It doesn't look real," she said to Jean-Claude.

"What does, anymore?"

If there had been planes in ancient times, she thought, *they would have looked like this one.*

"This is the ghost of early morning," she replied.

"Why do you say that?"

"The plane is still beautiful. Undefiled."

"*C'est vrai.*" His voice was full of sadness.

"The last plane on earth." She might as well be looking at the stars, thought Valerie — at distant light reaching her eye after its journey of a thousand years. Only the plane's glow came from light that had shone before the attacks — the same light that Gerard had seen on an airplane's wings from the observation deck of a tower that had fallen.

You cannot go back, she thought. *You cannot undo what has happened.*

"We must go," said Jean-Claude.

"Someone'll hear the engines," said Valerie. "So close to the airport."

"They will not."

"With all the surveillance?"

"They will not hear them," he insisted, "because they do not expect to hear them."

No one expected an attack, either, thought Valerie.

The plane looked ethereal, an unfocused haze of light. She put her hand on the fuselage. Metallic and cool to the touch, its whiteness gleamed in the night air.

Jean-Claude gave her a boost, up into the cockpit. Climbing in on the pilot's side, he put on his headset and started flicking switches. The array of dials began to blink on, their needles swinging into position — fuel gauge, tachometer, artificial horizon — a green glow in the blackness, a numeric code as indecipherable as a lost language.

Andre, I love you.

The engine roared, crushing silence in its teeth, frothing up water as the plane rose over the cove.

* * *

We are alone in the sky.

The thought terrified Valerie as she peered into the blackness framed by the overhanging wing and the zigzag struts with their cut-out view of the night. She couldn't talk to Jean-Claude. The noise of the engine made talk impossible, even with the headset he'd given her. Then as she was gazing out into the darkness, she could feel the rumble of the plane as it entered her body, as it took on the rhythm of her pulse and heartbeat. *We are alone in the sky,* the rumbling said. The noise grew louder and louder until it crashed and broke on her ears.

The engines cut out. The vibrations stopped.

Then came silence. It was profound, and it held everything in its depths, as if it were rich soil, seeded with life. *No one could find us inside this silence,* thought Valerie. Radar could beam on them, its array of enormous dishes waiting to receive the echo of signals bouncing back, but she felt certain that this ghostlike plane would evade detection. Yet it troubled her to imagine a breakdown of radar — how one by one, each dish might quit its slow, deliberate scanning of the sky, how each might become a cartoon of itself yawning and stretching, softening into collapse. Perhaps their attackers had found some way to make this happen.

Valerie didn't believe that Jean-Claude had rediscovered the *système de pilotage* — flying on pirate beacons, communicating with blacked-out towers, sending encoded signals on lost radio bands, keeping the two of them hidden. She believed that no one was paying attention to these tiny islands and the sky above them. *In any case, the worst has already happened,* she thought, as if the day's allotment of cruelty had been used up. She felt no danger.

Static crackled in her headset. *"Notre belle terre,"* said Jean-Claude.

Our beautiful earth.

She looked down. They were flying along the archipelago of Saint-Pierre et Miquelon, its luminous geography etched into the glassy sea, but even though she could recognize its contours, she couldn't penetrate its strangeness. She wondered what made it so, even as they headed northward, bearing east, passing above a shoreline full of tiny lights, the gleam and twinkle of the town of Saint-Pierre. Valerie imagined the settlement below as a sky full of starry constellations — the lit shapes of houses and bistros, *gendarmerie* and harbour, *quais* jutting out like small, bright fists into the water. She felt upside-down, as if she were tethered to a spaceship, drifting above the stars of a lonely earth.

"Yes," she said. "It is beautiful."

The town slipped away as they moved northeast, flying above the shore road, above the waters of L'Anse Coudreville. This was the inlet she'd seen from the hills in the early morning, but no, it was not; she'd never again see L'Anse Coudreville as it was at the moment when James had been on his way to the tower restaurant in New York and Chantal was striding off to a working lunch in Paris and she herself was crouching on her knees, camera aimed at tiny flowers, frail and growing low to the rocky ground. How precious these human conjunctions were, those meandering thoughts, these silvery spheres of light, these ghosts that cannot be brought back.

Absences made everything looked strange to her.

"No one can find us here," Jean-Claude said.

They were flying in figure eights around the archipelago, over open water westward toward Langlade, an island hitched by a slender thread of sand to the largest of the chain, Mique-lon, as if sand were flowing from one to the other, the two forming an hourglass. West across the neck of the hourglass they flew; northward along the west coast of Miquelon, making an eastward loop around Le Cap at the northern tip of the island, then heading south along its eastern coast. She saw the brittle etching of shapes against water, broken shards of waves hitting rock, their scattered light gleaming. Now they were completing the figure eight, flying westward across the neck of the hourglass, southward along the west coast of Langlade. She wondered if the northernmost island of Miquelon might disappear, its sand pouring through the narrow spit to the smaller island below it.

We've run out of time, said Charlie Reilly.

She wasn't even sure what time was. Or direction. Eastwest-northsouth, the oscillating of gyrocompasses, slamming planes into buildings. A thing no human being would countenance. The plane headed eastward, back toward Saint-Pierre.

Jean-Claude was talking on his radio.

She'd forgotten to call Marguerite.

She wondered where Gerard was.

At some point, she must have slept.

They were gliding above open water, the Gulf of St. Lawrence.

She watched Jean-Claude as he radioed whatever tower was guiding them. Yet as she looked at him, she saw a stranger, a man inhabited by a need for silence, and she thought of poor Mr. Groves, that lost soul who longed for tranquillity, a hope that once again had vanished from the earth.

* * *

Matt, what do you think happened to that guy?

I think he took off, is what I think.

They were sitting on his back stoop. Valerie was plucking her guitar.

You think he's alive?

Yup.

Don't you think that's kind of a creepy thing to do?

What, you mean run off?

Valerie felt impatient. *I mean, not telling anyone where you're off to.*

Matt paused. He took a long, low breath. *After what he'd been through, I guess you should sort of expect it.*

But he had a family. They loved him.

They loved him in another world, said Matt. *That world is gone.*

* * *

There are two worlds then, she'd said to Gerard when he came home from Rwanda. *There's the branch that for years is whole and then there's the same branch that snaps and breaks in a hurricane. You can't go back and fix it.*

It is like that, chère *Valerie,* he replied.

Even though I love you.

You loved me before it happened, he said.

Are you saying I can't love you now?

Hesitant, he reached out to embrace her, as if she were nothing but shadows, as if he were blind.

* * *

On the stoop with Matthew, she had plucked out the chords, the notes of a song. The melody kept running through her head.

* * *

Those men with the knives, those hijackers killed my father, who was found this morning, lying face down in the brackish waters of the pond. It's the truth. Lift the constraints of time, and you will see that those same murderers twisted the mind of Charlie Reilly and set it ticking like a bomb, the sound so loud that I could hear it coming from the horlogerie *as I walked this morning on the Rue Maréchal Foch. Maybe what I heard wasn't the sound of clocks at all, but of a human pulse, the thudding of terrified hearts, the voices of those about to die.*

Laurent Sarazin was dead by then.

Matt still wears his father's ancient wristwatch. He wore it this morning.

At eight forty-six a.m., Eastern Daylight Time, the watch stopped.

* * *

Peering into the darkness, she glimpsed Gerard, high above the city, standing at the confluence of two great rivers. He was taking a picture for her. A shot of James, stepping into the elevator. Another of Andre walking into the lobby, laptop on his shoulder.

What you remember is still here. Nothing ever vanishes.

It is happening now, unfolding before me.

How brave of Jean-Claude, to open his heart to the sky.

Through her headset, she heard him. "Let us defy them all," he said.

* * *

Andre and James, I lift up my eyes to the hills. I feel you in the mystery of this night, in the air's cool touch on my hand. Flower in the crannied wall, precious children, I pluck you out of the towers' crannies. I hold you, root and all, in my hand.

Andre, Andre.

I cannot know anything at all.

46

W HEN THE PLANE SPLASHED down at Étang du Cap Noir,
Valerie had no idea of the time, no sense of where she
was. Her watch had stopped and she couldn't get her bear-
ings from the sky. Odd constellations sketched themselves
against the blackness, a dusty crumble of unfamiliar stars.
It must be very late, she thought. She had no idea how long
they'd flown.

"You slept," said Jean-Claude.

"Some of the time."

"It was magnificent," he said.

"Yes," she replied. "It was." Valerie glanced at the plane,
as if it might disappear.

"*Chère* Valerie, whatever you've seen has vanished."

"Nothing vanishes."

"Does it give you hope, to know that?"

"All day long I've seen my son. Even as we flew."

"I did not see my brother."

"Yes, but there's still no word—"

"What happened is unspeakable. That is why there is no
word." He took her hands. "I want to vanish into silence,"
he said.

"But you just did."

"No. I flew to make restitution to the dead. There is nothing
more I can do."

"But we found—"

"Whatever we imagined." He reached to embrace her, but she pulled away from him.

"Don't frighten me," she said.

"How am I frightening you?"

"Please don't come near me. If you touch me, I'll collapse."

"But you need—"

"—My son alive," she said.

* * *

Valerie could sense that Jean-Claude was afraid to leave her alone, and she watched as he turned away, knowing he'd keep an eye on her from the scant shelter of a few sparse trees. She could feel terror slithering through her body, its hold on her warm and seductive. *No. It'll put me to sleep. It'll smother me.*

She tore off her clothes, ran into the chill ache of the pond, went under and began to swim, and then she felt the silver band slipping from her wrist, but she let it go, treading cold water until her body's aching turned to numbness. Alone she wept, afraid of the salt heat of her tears. She held her breath and went under until the tears stopped. Safe again, she swam back to shore.

* * *

Jean-Claude had left his backpack on the dock. Valerie opened it, found a towel and dried herself off. She got dressed and looked around. He was nowhere in sight. At least she couldn't see him.

She slumped down, face in her hands, exhausted. Images drifted through her head — guttering candles in Union Square, placards in many languages. *Si vous avez des renseignements ... If you have information....* Gerard had written a phone number on the sign. Maybe she'd imagined the names. *Andre Jean Lefèvre. James Eliot Wilson.* Sleep nudged her eyes into closing.

A sweet melody, Beethoven's "Für Elise," her mother's hands on the piano, then her voice. *Come and sit beside me, Valerie.*

She woke up and answered her phone.

"*Allô?*" She was shaking like a tree about to fall. "*Gerard?*" She listened.

"*Ma chère Valerie...*" he began. "*Je suis desolé.*"

"*Tu as des nouvelles?*" You have news?

Dust she became, as she blew into the wind.

Then came darkness. Then she felt nothing at all.

* * *

When she returned to the *pension* in Saint-Pierre, Valerie went to bed and slept for twenty-four hours, erasing the twelfth of September 2001 from the page of memory. When she got up and went to make the bed, she found under her pillow a lavender sachet. Apart from that detail, she remembered almost nothing. She didn't recognize Marguerite's garden. Its brilliant yellow flowers, its pendulous squash and fragrant herbs had lost all depth, had collapsed into a lifeless surface, as charming and bland as a greeting card. It didn't matter.

She spent the day making arrangements to leave the island, and the following morning, an officer in *képi* and white gloves rapped on the door of the *pension* on Rue Amiral Mueslier. The gendarme was not Lisette's brother-in-law, but his commanding officer, a captain. He was there to drive Madame Lefèvre to the airport, as a compassionate gesture from the government of France. The captain held out his arm, escorted Valerie down the stairs and helped her into the car. She couldn't recall saying goodbye to Marguerite or Robert, but she felt sure she must have done so.

They would drive down Rue Amiral Muselier, passing one by one the rakish clapboard houses on the street. It would feel to Valerie as if she were looking at pictures, as if this street no longer existed, as if the lively blue *pension*, trimmed in red and painted by Robert with such affection, had drawn its curtains, pulled down its shades, and died. It sat as still as a travel poster for a place she'd never been.

Then she noticed Marguerite and Robert. They were standing at the front door, grave sentinels keeping watch. Valerie thought of a lighthouse, its rotating beams. Then she imagined night, the two of them visible to all the ships at sea.

Epilogue

VALERIE REMEMBERS EVERYTHING. She imagines a river in flood, the East River about to wash out the Brooklyn Bridge, this secluded park, this momentary peace. She's seated, holding the hand of white-haired Gerard who looks older than his years. It's late summer and there will be no flood, only a mist of soft rain, only the wrought-iron lanterns, gas-lit even in daylight, only the strangeness of this garden lush with rhododendron shrubs, the Manhattan sky as grey and soft as a cat. Time is passing, and memory drifts at the edge of time.

Six years ago, they were lost in ashes and tolling bells, in candles and murmured prayers. They'd gone to a service at a Catholic church in the Village to mourn with the friends of Andre and James. Chantal and her husband flew in from Paris; Gerard's brother came from Montreal. Karen and her partner took care of everyone, and afterwards they all went home to sweep up the shards of grief, to dispose of them as safely as they could.

Yet Valerie remembered how Jean-Claude's presence had brought hope that the vanished might return, how their flight together was a blessing on the sky, how in spite of their anguish, they'd touched each other with kindness. She wondered if she and Gerard could once again be gentle with each other, if she could talk to him in the depths of his suffering.

It didn't turn out as she'd expected. On their first evening back in Toronto, Gerard took both her hands in his. She was sitting and he knelt down, kissed her hands and said, *Please forgive me, Valerie for what I've made you suffer. Life has taught me what is important, it was always you and Chantal and Andre, and now that I have lost our son, I feel I am about to lose you, too.*

Valerie hid her face in her hands. Words fled her as if she were on fire — her sanity in ashes, as Gerard's had been. She remembered how many times he'd poured scotch into a glassful of ice and silence, and she wept. He knelt beside her, put his arms around her, held her and whispered, *Je comprends, je comprends.* I understand, but also *I know how you feel, I realize.*

And he did — she knew that. Much as she'd guessed at his infidelities, he'd feel in her body the longing that Jean-Claude could have satisfied, the place she'd cleansed of Gerard's absences, of his constant game of cards with Death where he'd pocket the proceeds for a night or two with her. He knew he'd almost lost her, she could sense it. Even so, he didn't have to bend down and kiss the hollow that another man had longed to fill. Didn't have to murmur, once again, *forgive me* when life had been so cruel to him, first his son and then his wife who'd imagined fleeing if the worst should happen.

* * *

From: Matthew Reilly
Subject: Condolences
1 September 2002

Dear Valerie,
I know that this email will come as a surprise, since we have not been in touch for a very long time. Quite by accident, I learned from a mutual friend about your tragedy. It is shameful

that I never wrote, never called. After the attacks, I decided to remain a priest. It was just as well. I wasn't generous enough to give you the consolation that you needed. I wasn't even brave enough to pick up the phone and tell you that.

I don't believe that God saved my life so that I could do some special work. Who was lost and who was saved is no more or less meaningful than what happens when a hurricane blows through a field of flowers. We are here by the grace of God. We come and go by the wind of time, and that is all.

I'm a priest because I have my limits, not because I believe more fervently than anyone else.

Please give my best to Gerard. I hold you and your family in prayer.

With best wishes,
Matthew Reilly

* * *

Valerie knew that Matthew had survived by missing his plane. She couldn't have avoided knowing it — his story was on the news, but she'd been too distraught to pay much attention. Yet she felt there was something she'd left undone and after she received Matt's letter, she sent him a prayer card from the service held in New York City for her son. It read:

In Loving Memory of Andre J. Lefèvre
18 February 1971-11 September 2001

It was the first date that mattered, but she thought no more about it until Gerard read a report online in *The Boston Globe* about the city's observances on the first anniversary. They'd mentioned Matt's homily based on a text from the Book of Job, *and only I alone have escaped to tell you*, a text he used because he wanted to bear witness to the suffering of parents who lost children on that day, but no one knew he was talking about his own son, and no one knew what grief he felt, if any.

* * *

"You didn't sleep well last night?" asks Gerard.

"It is six years."

He's silent. "What is a year?" he says at last.

* * *

What is a year? It's always the same. On each anniversary they'd go to Andre's old church in the Village, attend a service, stroll down West Broadway, pick up a deli sandwich, find a bench in Battery Park or along the Hudson River promenade to the west of the ruined towers, and then they'd lose themselves in a long meander through the same questions, the same reminiscences, a treadmill of rumination that Valerie understood to be a form of grieving, so that this year she said, *Let's go to City Hall Park, away from the crowds. It won't feel as sad there.* Only now she wonders how she could have thought that. It wasn't as if they'd fled downtown Manhattan. They are sitting just a kilometre away from the place where they'd lost their son.

What is a year? Gerard had asked.

"Years are to time," says Valerie, "what bureau drawers are to clothing."

"To keep experience tidy," he replies.

"It's just a convention."

"But I need to believe in years," says Gerard.

His tone of voice makes the air tremble. She turns to look at him. *I must keep sane somehow,* his eyes say.

* * *

Your eyes said more than that, Gerard. They said, I've seen what can't be borne, *because your eyes speak with fierce elo-*

quence when you cannot speak in any other way. I knew this in our youth and yet I never understood it. I always thought that in time, words would follow a look of suffering because you were adept with words. This never happened. The night I flew with Jean-Claude, when I sat half-asleep on the dock at Étang de Cap Noir, my phone played "Für Elise" and you called and told me everything you didn't know — not with words, but with the sound of your voice. I fell as if into deep water, into every echo that the sound of your voice contained.

That morning you'd covered the disaster from a water-taxi bobbing around the tip of Manhattan, and as you moved westward toward the Hudson, your cameraman was shooting; he had a telephoto lens on his rig, a zoom, and he let you look through it toward the burning towers, the southmost one from which Andre had called you, and you saw specks of humanity floating like ash into the sky. You felt sick with disgust, as if the act of looking might honour the destruction forced on these victims, and so you turned away from the videocam, handing it back to your cameraman, and then you felt a humming in your pocket. It was your phone, and you knew without asking who it was.

"But I saw him alive," *I interrupted.*

"Forgive me, chère Valerie. I, too, was convinced he was alive. I imagined him running down the stairs as we spoke. I did not want to believe, but then..."

"But how can you be sure...?"

"He said, Je t'aime, papa. And that he loved you, too. He could not get through to Saint-Pierre."

"But he did, Gerard. I saw the two of them in the Place de L'Église."

"Mon pauvre," *you said.*

"All day I was certain. I was so sure he made it."

"All day I lied to myself, Valerie."

* * *

Remembering this, Gerard sits forward, his face in his hands and Valerie rubs his back. She always rubs his back when he speaks like this, as if she could ease the knot of grief in his body. *That sign you saw on TV, I had to do it,* he'd said. *I knew you'd be watching the vigil. I wanted so much to have hope. I didn't want to know the truth myself.* She remembers that night, that conversation, how Jean-Claude came and took her back to the *pension,* how kind Marguerite and Robert had been, how they'd looked after everything when she had to leave for New York. She wonders what they'd think of the city. Marguerite, she feels certain, would admire City Hall Park, its jungle of lush rhododendron shrubs, their long leaves glistening. Robert would feel at home with the moody coastal weather, knowing better than to check the forecast. Earlier this morning, there'd been showers. Warm, soft rain.

* * *

"Come, let's walk," says Valerie.

Gerard gets up, and the two of them make their way through garden paths, admiring the elegant wrought-iron gaslights, the glossy shrubbery, the flower beds near City Hall.

"Do you remember your garden?" she asks.

Gerard is silent. "I'd rather not," he says at last.

"It inspired me."

"But you are a true gardener," he says. "You have hope."

"And you don't?"

"I am not so patient."

"You weren't happy when you gardened. That's all."

"And now flowers remind me of death," he says.

Valerie pauses. "You've never told me that."

"I'm telling you now."

"How sad. Flowers console me."

"*Que Dieu te bénisse.*" His laugh is tart. "Imagination is as good as a stiff drink, *ma pauvre Valerie.*"

"Gerard." She hears her voice break.

"What, *ma chère?*"

"Does nothing console you?"

* * *

It's a foolish question. We've had to struggle, mourning Andre and forgiving each other at the same time, and it has been hard and painful. Forgiveness is nothing more than the shape you give your life — you are a forgiving person or you are not. In marriage, you open your body to tenderness and human failing. We knew the frailty of our relationship, and we knew it might break and fall apart under the weight of grief.

Yet a child's murder is so terrible a thing that even estranged spouses have mercy on each other; even in our regret, we had to acknowledge the love and support of Chantal and our son-in-law, the presence of our new grandchild. We had to accept that too much happens in the life of a family, much of it inexpressible.

Too many lost souls gather and abide with us. And then they depart, as unconsoled as we are, for we have life and they do not.

So you are not consoled, Gerard — I understand. As for myself, wary and uncertain about love, I look at the empty sky where those towers were. Everything leaves us, says the void. Everything remains.

* * *

"I do not feel hopeless," says Gerard. "It is just that — I loved my son."

"*Je comprends. Bien sûr.*"

"Ask me next year, how I am." His smile is sad.

* * *

When Andre died, Ora died all over again, you told me that. Only this time, everything changed. You stopped drinking, you cut back on your work, and now you're an anchor on local French TV; desk work, no reporting — a man whose penetrating gaze has witnessed its final act of savagery. Nowadays, you don't know what to make of the world, of its grave injustice. You look at me with fearful eyes, as if you could never be certain of anything again.

I try to reassure you, but not with words. About this tragedy, far too many words have already been said. You need to know that because of your tenderness, Andre was born, when he might not have been. Because of your compassion, he had thirty years of life. So I return to you what you gave my son. I touch your face — your eyes, your lips. With my hands I turn your gaze toward me so that you may look into my eyes and see him.

* * *

Valerie gazes at the New York City sky, and then she drifts into its greyness, seeing invisible boats, hearing the clank of rigging in the *barachois* — early morning in the town of Saint-Pierre, the steep island street as it was before everything happened.

In City Hall Park, Gerard takes her hand between his, and in its warmth, she feels an infinite strangeness. There's no sense to be made of anything. Sense isn't the point, she thinks. Life is too mysterious for sense.

"You never know," she says.

"Know what?"

She can hear an engine's purr grow louder, and then she sees a small plane threading itself through the haze; in, then out, like a needle through silk. The plane's headed east, toward LaGuardia.

225

"It may be Mr. Groves."
Gerard looks at her, and his face softens.
"You wrote a song about him once."
"Trying to come home," she says.

Acknowledgements

I would like to thank the Canada Council for the Arts for their generous support of this project. A warm thank you to my publisher Luciana Ricciutelli for her wholehearted and generous response to this work. Long after my travels in the year 2000, I want to acknowledge Nicole and Jean Lerolland, whose *pension* on the island of St. Pierre bore rich soil for the seed of this novel. *Merci pour votre gentillesse.* The mysterious clay vessel that Valerie discovers was inspired by the work of Israeli ceramist Judith Halfon. Thank you to Irene Guilford and Elizabeth Kaplan for reading earlier drafts of the manuscript and providing me with helpful insights and suggestions. And heartfelt thanks to you, Brian, my friend and companion at every stage of this long but fruitful journey.

Photo: Jorjas Photography

Carole Giangrande's two most recent books, the novellas *Here Comes The Dreamer* and *Midsummer,* were both published by Inanna Publications. A previous novella, *A Gardener On The Moon,* won the 2010 Ken Klonsky Novella Contest. She's the author of the novels, *An Ordinary Star* (2004) and *A Forest Burning* (2000), and a short story collection, *Missing Persons* (1994), as well as two non-fiction books: *Down To Earth: The Crisis in Canadian Farming* (1985) and *The Nuclear North: The People, The Regions and the Arms Race* (1983). She's worked as a broadcast journalist for CBC Radio, and her fiction, poetry, articles and reviews have appeared in literary journals and in Canada's major newspapers. Visit her website at www.carolegiangrande.com.